POKÉMON™
BLACK & WHITE
POCKET COMICS
STORY & AR
SANTA
D0057873

POKÉMON TYPE MATCHUP CHART

Pokémon Quizzes begin on page 5! Test your knowledge of Pokémon strengths and weaknesses. Study up by taking a good close look at the Type Chart, conveniently located on page 3!

The effect of a Pokémon move in battle depends on the type of the attacking Pokémon's move and the type of the defending Pokémon.

① Pokémon moves are separated into types.

BLITZLE ATTACKS WITH SPARK, AN ELECTRIC-TYPE MOVE!

② Depending on the type of the defending Pokémon...

DRILBUR
Ground type

SNIVY
Grass type

TEPIG
Fire type

OSHAWOTT
Water type

③ ...the effect of the move will vary!

No Effect | Not very effective | Normal effect | Super effective

TYPE MATCHUP CHART	Defending Pokémon's Type																
Attacking Pokémon's Move Type	Normal	Fire	Water	Electric	Grass	Ice	Fighting	Poison	Ground	Flying	Psychic	Bug	Rock	Ghost	Dragon	Dark	Steel
Normal													△	×			△
Fire		△	△		○	○						○	△		△		○
Water		○	△		△				○				○		△		
Electric			○	△	△				×	○					△		
Grass		△	○		△			△	○	△		△	○		△		△
Ice		△	△		○	△			○	○					○		△
Fighting	○					○		△		△	△	△	○	×		○	○
Poison					○			△	△				△	△			×
Ground		○		○	△			○		×		△	○				○
Flying				△	○		○					○	△				△
Psychic							○	○			△					×	△
Bug		△			○		△	△		△	○			△		○	△
Rock		○				○	△		△	○		○					△
Ghost	×										○			○		△	△
Dragon															○		△
Dark							△				○			○		△	△
Steel		△	△	△		○							○				△

LEGEND

○ = Super effective

△ = Not very effective

× = No effect

No mark = Normal effect

If the defending Pokémon has two types, then the effect of the move is calculated using both types. However, if either one of those types is No Effect (×), then the move will have no effect.

ARCHEOPS

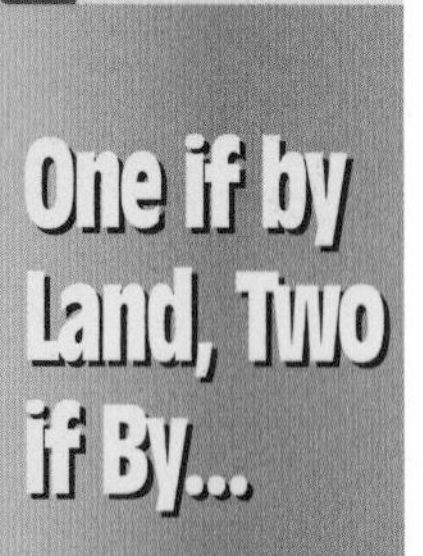
One if by Land, Two if By...

Whoosh...
Aaaaaaaaah!

Pokémon Black and White Quiz Answer.

Answer ?

flap flap
ARCHEOPS, WHY ARE YOU RUNNING?
BECAUSE I'M BETTER AT RUNNING THAN FLYING!

Starting with page 6, you'll find the answer to the quiz from the previous page here—plus an explanation!

AND IF I DON'T HURRY, I'M GOING TO BE LATE FOR THE POKÉMON MUSICAL AT NIMBASA CITY!
THAT'S NOT WHAT I MEANT...
YOU CAN'T WALK—OR RUN—ON WATER. AND THAT'S THE OCEAN UNDER YOU!
Now you tell me!!
Whoa...
Splash
POKÉMON BLACK & WHITE QUIZ
Archeops' Ability is Defeatist. What does it do?
1
Makes Archeops run away from battle when its HP is below 50%.
2
Makes Archeops' stats fall when its HP is below 50%.
3
Makes Archeops play dead when its HP is below 50%.

Unova Pokédex No.072

ARCHEN

I Hate When That Happens

Quiz answer for page 5.

Answer 2

Archeops are very powerful Pokémon, but they give up easily if they get hurt.

Pokémon
Black & White
Quiz
flap
flap
flap
flap
Aaaagh...
Archen is said to be the ancestor of all Flying-type Pokémon. What category is it?
1
Ancient Bird Pokémon
2
Beginning Bird Pokémon
3
First Bird Pokémon
Sproing
Whoa! Archen is flying!
I STUBBED MY TOE!!

Unova Pokédex No.138
DURANT
Longcut
Quiz answer for page 7.
Answer 3
Archen is the First Bird Pokémon.
WE'RE GOING TO HAVE TO GO AROUND THE MOUNTAIN TO GET TO THE NEXT TOWN.
BUT IT'S THE ONLY WAY TO TOWN.
THAT'S SUCH A LONG WAY...
MAP
WAIT! I DUG A TUNNEL THROUGH THE MOUNTAIN!

Mountain
Exit
En-
trance
I MADE A SHORT-CUT!
IT'S A MAZE. I LIKE MAZES. THEY'RE AMAZING.
IT WOULD BE QUICKER TO TAKE THE LONG WAY AROUND!!
POKéMON
BLACK & WHITE
QUIZ
Durant create their nests by digging tunnels in mountains. Which Pokémon is their natural enemy?
1
Heatmor
2
Drilbur
3
Woobat

Unova Pokédex No.123
ACCELGOR
Dry Wit
Quiz answer for page 9.
Answer 1
WELL...? WHAT DO YOU THINK?! ISN'T IT COOL?
IT'S HOT TODAY. HOT AND DRY.
*Dry up
To avoid dehydration, Accelgor wraps its body in many layers of a thin membrane.
COOL? NO! IT'S TOO HOT AND DRY! I'M AFRAID OF DRYING UP!!
I DON'T WANT TO DRY UP*!!
Durant and Heatmor don't get along at all.
(10)

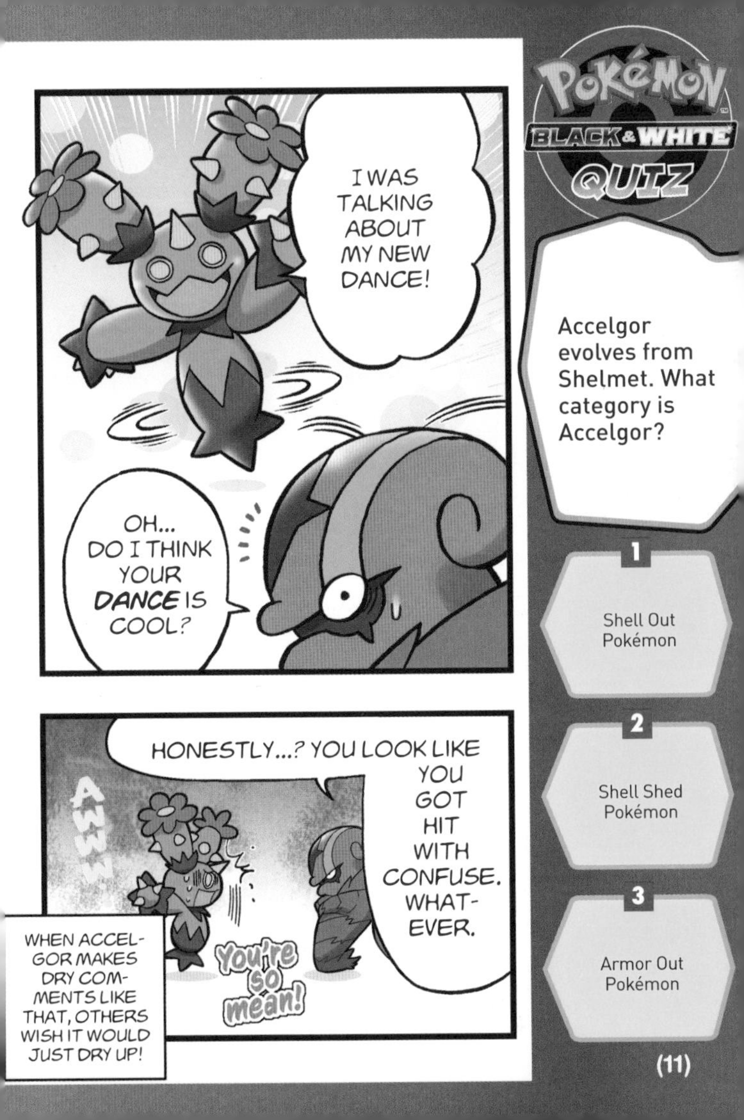
POKÉMON
BLACK & WHITE
QUIZ
I WAS TALKING ABOUT MY NEW DANCE!
OH... DO I THINK YOUR DANCE IS COOL?
HONESTLY...? YOU LOOK LIKE YOU GOT HIT WITH CONFUSE. WHAT-EVER.
AWWW
You're so mean!
WHEN ACCEL-GOR MAKES DRY COM-MENTS LIKE THAT, OTHERS WISH IT WOULD JUST DRY UP!
Accelgor evolves from Shelmet. What category is Accelgor?
1
Shell Out Pokémon
2
Shell Shed Pokémon
3
Armor Out Pokémon

CARRACOSTA

Yummy for My Tummy

Quiz answer for page 11.

Answer 1

Accelgor is the Shell Out Pokémon, which evolves from Shelmet, a Pokémon that has a shell.

Pokémon Black & White Quiz

Which of the following is true of Carracosta?

1

It is strong enough to create a hole in the bottom of a tanker with a single slap.

2

It spends its whole life at the bottom of the sea. It never ventures out on land.

3

It has no teeth, so it feeds on moss that grows on rocks.

Unova Pokédex No.063

DWEBBLE

Wherever You Go, There You Are

Quiz answer for page 13.

Answer 1

Carracosta is famous for its strength and powerful jaw. It can bite through steel beams and rocks.

POKÉMON
BLACK & WHITE
QUIZ
AT HOME, I GUESS...
HMM... WHAT ABOUT THE DAY BEFORE?
Home
STILL AT HOME, I GUESS...
DWEBBLE IS ALWAYS AT HOME.
Dwebble carves a hole in a rock to wear and live in. How does it create the hole?
1
It uses its sharp claws and spends years working away at it.
2
It searches the beach for rocks with holes worn out by the waves.
3
It secretes a liquid out of its mouth that metts a hole into the rock.

CRUSTLE

Mobile Home

THAT'S A FINE LOOKING HOUSE YOU'VE GOT THERE.
OH, HI!

Quiz answer for page 15.

Answer 3

WHY, THANK YOU. BUT IT'S TOO BIG FOR JUST ME.
SO I'M RENTING OUT THE UPSTAIRS.

Dwebble secretes a liquid out of its mouth that melts rocks so that it can easily and quickly create hidey-holes.

POKéMON BLACK & WHITE QUIZ

The following are Rock-type Pokémon. Which one is the heaviest?

1

Crustle

2

Boldore

3

Carracosta

BRAVIARY

Instrumental in Its Demise

Quiz answer for page 17.

Answer 1

Crustle weighs in as the heaviest at 440.9 lbs. Boldore weighs 224.9 lbs. and Carracosta weighs 178.6 lbs.

POKÉMON BLACK & WHITE QUIZ

Braviary is a dual-type Pokémon. Which one of these Pokémon has exactly the same types as Braviary?

1 Tornadus

2 Archeops

3 Unfezant

VOLCARONA

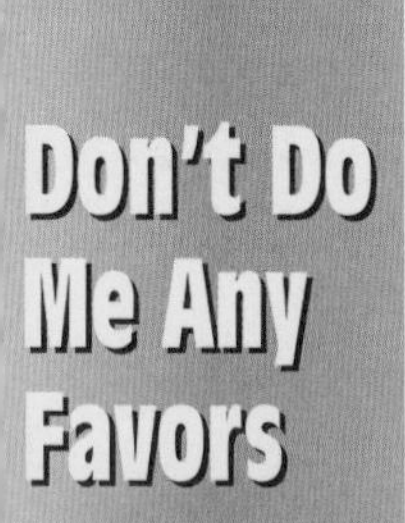

Don't Do Me Any Favors

Quiz answer for page 19.

Answer 3

A LONG TIME AGO... WHEN THIS PLANET WAS CLOAKED IN DARKNESS BECAUSE OF THE VOLCANIC ASH FILLING ITS ATMO-SPHERE...
...IT IS SAID THAT VOLCARONA REPLACED THE SUN TO PROVIDE LIGHT FOR EVERY-ONE.

I WANT TO GET A REALLY NICE SUNTAN BEFORE THE SUMMER'S OVER...
SO GO AHEAD AND *LET IT SHINE*, SUNSHINE!
OKAY...

Braviary is a Normal- and Flying-type Pokémon. Unfezant is also a Normal- and Flying-type Pokémon.

POKÉMON BLACK & WHITE QUIZ
FWHOOSH!
AAAAH. OWWWWW?! WHAT THE...?
Volcarona has the Flame Body Ability. What category of Pokémon is it?
1
Blazing Pokémon
2
Brutal Pokémon
3
Sun Pokémon
WARNING: DIRECT EXPOSURE TO VOLCARONA LIGHT CAN BE DANGEROUS!
SIZZLE SIZZLE
SIZZLE
SUNTAN, SUNBURN... WHAT'S THE DIF'? AT LEAST I'M NOT ALL PASTY WHITE ANYMORE, RIGHT?

EMOLGA

Go Fly A...

Quiz answer for page 21.

Answer 3

Volcarona is the Sun Pokémon, Darmanitan is the Blazing Pokémon and Hydreigon is the Brutal Pokémon.

YOU'RE FLYING EMOLGA LIKE A KITE?!
WHY'RE YOU GIVING ME THAT LOOK...?!

tup
Hello ...!
What?
OF COURSE NOT... CAN YOU HEAR ME, EMOLGA?
YES, I CAN HEAR YOU. OVER AND OUT!
OH! IT'S A TIN-CAN TELE-PHONE!!
POKÉMON BLACK & WHITE QUIZ
Where does Emolga, an Electric- and Flying-type Pokémon, store its electricity?
1
Under its cape-like skin.
2
In its cheek pouches.
3
In its tail.

Unova Pokédex No.053

WHIMSICOTT

Falling Through the Cracks

Quiz answer for page 23.

Answer 1

Emolga generates electricity in its cheek pouches and stores it inside its cape-like skin.

Stare
Pokémon Black & White Quiz
Whimsicott can enter a house through the tiniest cracks. What does it do once it's inside?
?
1 Makes mischief
2 Naps
3 Eats
I love you! But you slipped through...
...my fingers ♡
YOU JUST BROKE MY HEART...
WHIMSICOTT CAN SLIP THROUGH ALL KINDS OF TIGHT SPACES...

EMBOAR

All Fired up

Quiz answer for page 25.

Answer 1

Whimsicott enter your house with mischief on their mind.

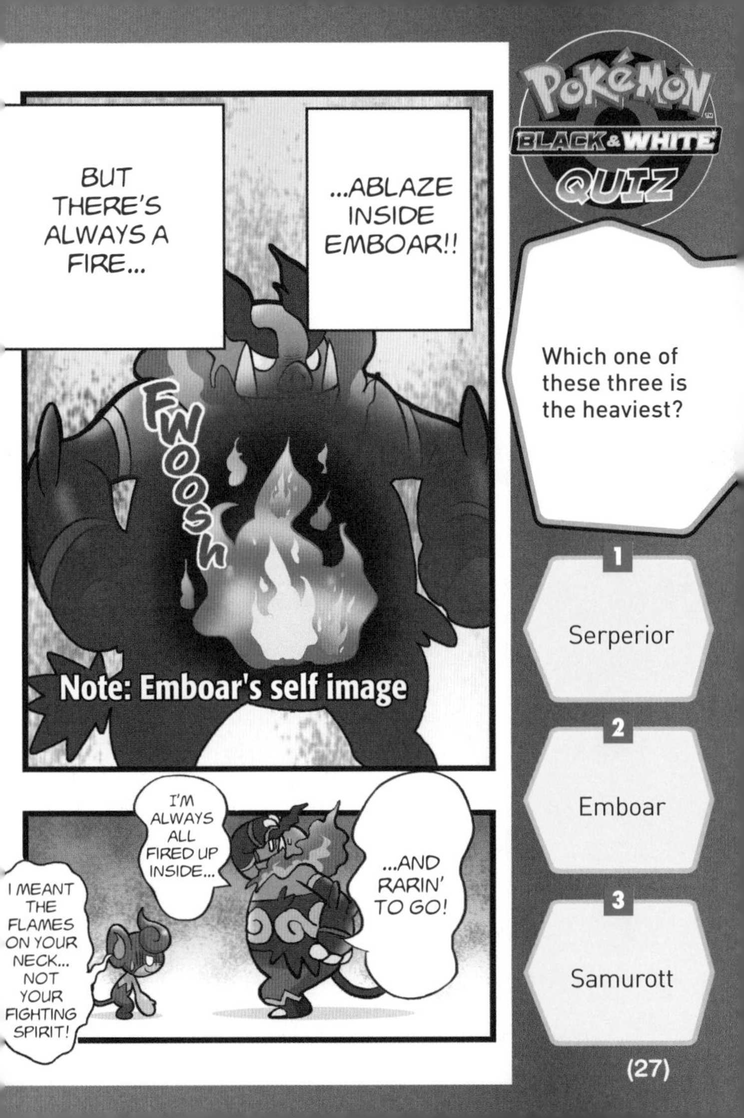
BUT THERE'S ALWAYS A FIRE...
...ABLAZE INSIDE EMBOAR!!
FWOOSH
Note: Emboar's self image
I'M ALWAYS ALL FIRED UP INSIDE...
...AND RARIN' TO GO!
I MEANT THE FLAMES ON YOUR NECK... NOT YOUR FIGHTING SPIRIT!
POKÉMON BLACK & WHITE QUIZ
Which one of these three is the heaviest?
1 Serperior
2 Emboar
3 Samurott

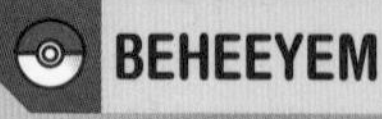

BEHEEYEM

Maid to Order

Quiz answer for page 27.

Answer 2

Emboar is the heaviest, at 330.7 lbs. Serperior weighs 138.9 lbs. and Samurott weighs 208.6 lbs.

Grrr
YES! YOU DISGUST ME, BEHEEYEM!!
YOU ABSOLUTELY, TOTALLY DISGUST ME!!
I SAID "CLEAN AND DUST" NOT "SCREAM" AND "DISGUST"!!
Bah.
POKÉMON
BLACK & WHITE
QUIZ
Beheeyem attacks with Psybeam. Which of these Pokémon does this move not affect?
1
Vullaby
2
Yamask
3
Minccino

TYMPOLE

Cold Shoulders

Quiz answer for page 29.

Answer 1

Psybeam is a Psychic-type move. It has no effect on Vullaby, a Dark-type Pokémon.

SCALD!!
glub glub glub
PANPOUR USES THE MOVE SCALD.
TA-DAH! NOW YOU TYMPOLE WILL FINALLY WARM UP TO ME!
NICE, HUH?
HEY! YOU TURNED OUR REFRESHING POND INTO A STEAMING BATH!! GRRR...
POKÉMON BLACK & WHITE QUIZ
Which of these Pokémon weighs the most?
1
Tympole
2
Emolga
3
Minccino

HAXORUS

Flower Power

Quiz answer for page 31.

Answer 3

Tympole weighs 9.9 lbs., Emolga weighs 11.0 lbs., and Minccino is the heaviest at 12.8 lbs.

POKéMON BLACK & WHITE QUIZ

Haxorus attacks with Guillotine. Which of these Pokémon will this move not affect?

FRAXURE

One Weigh to Do It

Quiz answer for page 33.

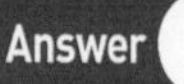

Answer 1

Guillotine is a Normal-type move. It has no effect on Frillish, a Ghost-type Pokémon.

Which of the following is true about Fraxure?

1

Their tusks grow back no matter how many times they break.

2

After a battle, they sharpen their tusks with a river rock.

3

Their tusks are detachable.

KARRABLAST

You Can Say Hat Again

Quiz answer for page 35.

Answer 2

Fraxure's tusks will not grow back if they break. They carefully sharpen their tusks using a river rock after battle.

HEY, SHELMET! WAIT!

KARRA-BLAST WANTS A CHAT!

A HAT? I DON'T HAVE A HAT!

I COVER MY HEAD WITH MY SHELL!

APPARENTLY IT COVERS YOUR **EARS** TOO...

POKÉMON BLACK & WHITE QUIZ

All of these Pokémon are 1'08" in height. Which of them is the heaviest?

Unova Pokédex No.042

PALPITOAD

I've Got This Problem Licked!

LOOKS LIKE YOU COULD USE SOME HELP!
YOU'RE RIGHT, PALPITOAD. WOULD YOU MIND GETTING THAT BERRY FOR ME?

NO PROBLEM!

Thwaaap

PALPITOAD USES ITS LONG, STICKY TONGUE TO CAPTURE ITS PREY!

Quiz answer for page 37.

Answer 2

Karrablast is 13.0 lbs. Swadloon is 16.1 lbs. and Petilil is 14.6 lbs. So Swadloon is the heaviest.

You are battling Palpitoad! Which one of these moves would be super effective?

1. Tepig's Flame Charge
2. Oshawott's Razor Shell
3. Snivy's Leaf Tornado

SEISMITOAD

A Jarring Discovery

Quiz answer for page 39.

Answer 3

Palpitoad is a Water- and Ground-type Pokémon, so Leaf Tornado, a Grass-type move, would be super effective against it.

Grrr
Hmph.
Aaargh!
MY HAND IS TOO BIG! I CAN'T GET IT OUT OF THE JAR!
WHAT ARE YOU DOING, SEISMI-TOAD?
HERE, GIVE IT TO ME...
Ta-dah!
PLOP
Why didn't I think of that?!
POKéMON BLACK & WHITE QUIZ
Which of these moves won't work on Seismitoad?
1
Flame Charge
2
Razor Shell
3
Spark

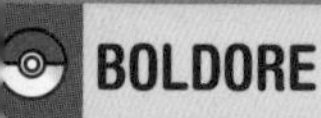

BOLDORE

Smack It to Me

Quiz answer for page 41.

Answer 3

Seismitoad is a Water- and Ground-type Pokémon. Spark, an Electric-type move, won't work against it.

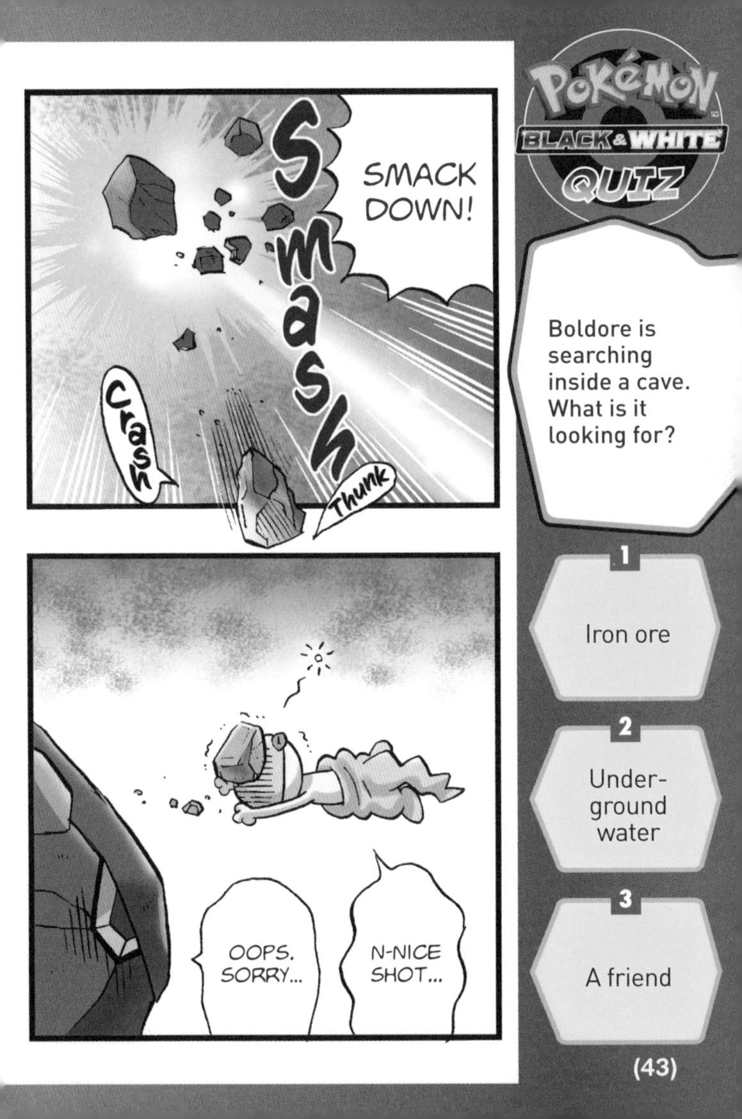

Pokémon
BLACK & WHITE
QUIZ
SMACK DOWN!
Smash
Crash
Thunk
N-NICE SHOT...
OOPS. SORRY...
Boldore is searching inside a cave. What is it looking for?
1
Iron ore
2
Under-ground water
3
A friend

KLINK

In the Klink

Quiz answer for page 43.

Answer 2

Boldore searches for underground water in caves.

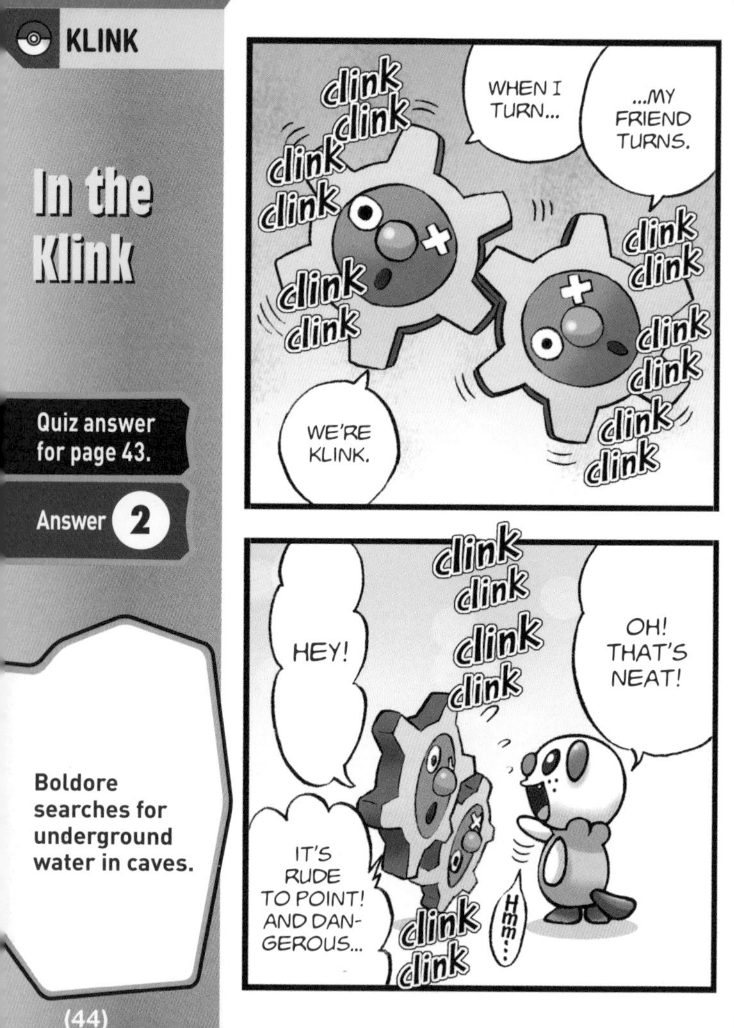

Pokémon
Black & White
Quiz
squish
klinkk... squish...
K-KLIIIIIIIIIIINK!!
I TRIED TO WARN YOU!
Why do Klink have two bodies that spin around each other?
1
To create energy.
2
To attack whatever approaches them.
3
To move in a different direction by changing the way they rotate.

GIGALITH

Mount a Protest

GIGALITH GATHERS SOLAR ENERGY INSIDE ITS BODY...
...AND THEN SHOOTS IT OUT FROM ITS MOUTH!!

Quiz answer for page 45.

Answer 1

AND THAT ENERGY...
FOOOM!
...IS POWERFUL ENOUGH TO...
...BLOW AWAY AN ENTIRE MOUNTAIN!!

Klink generate the energy they need to live by interlocking with each other's bodies and rotating.

twitch
twitch
twitch
H-
HEY...
HUH
?
IT'S ME,
GIGALITH!!
I'm not a mountain!!
SORRY...
YOU
LOOKED
LIKE ONE...
FROM A
DISTANCE...
WITHOUT MY
GLASSES...
POKÉMON
BLACK & WHITE
QUIZ
Gigalith's Ability is Sturdy. What does it do?
1
Opponents cannot inflict a critical hit.
2
Only super effective moves inflict damage.
3
Gigalith cannot be knocked out with one hit.

KLANG

Gearing Up

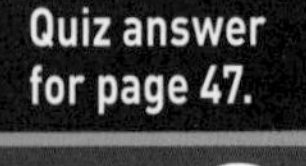

Quiz answer for page 47.

Answer 3

Sturdy prevents an opponent from knocking a Pokémon out with one hit when its HP is full.

KLANG SPINS ITS MINIGEAR EXTREMELY FAST BEFORE FIRING IT TOWARDS ITS OPPONENT.
click click click click

ALL RIGHT... GO, MINIGEAR!!
YOU CAN DO IT! I HAVE FAITH IN YOU!
B-BUT... I DON'T WANT TO!!

POKéMON
BLACK & WHITE
QUIZ
I'LL BE RIGHT BEHIND YOU, I PROMISE. TRUST ME.
THAT'S WHAT YOU ALWAYS SAY!
What emotion makes Klang spin faster?
FWOOSH!
OH, HI, LILLIGANT. UMM... WILL YOU GO OUT WITH ME?
HUH?
1
Happiness
2
Sadness
3
Anger

KLINKLANG

Spin Cycle

click click click click

click click click click

click click click click

WHAT THE...?

Quiz answer for page 49.

Answer 3

The angrier it gets, the faster Klang spins.

POKÉMON BLACK & WHITE QUIZ

What does the red core of Klinklang do?

1. It flashes to indicate danger to others.
2. It is a tank to store energy.
3. It shoots out laser beams.

AXEW

Talk About Bed Head!

Quiz answer for page 51.

Answer 2

Klinklang stores the energy it generates inside its red core. This energy can be shot out from its spikes.

MY TUSK GOT STUCK IN MY PILLOW.
I can't get it out... Sniffle.

Which of the following is true about Axew, the Tusk Pokémon?

1

They crush rocks with their tusks and eat them.

2

If their tusks break, new ones grow back.

3

Their tusks can expand and contract.

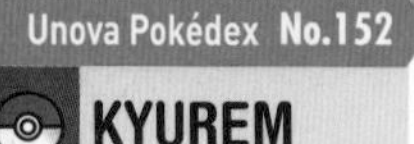

A Chilly Reception

Quiz answer for page 53.

Answer 2

Axew's tusks grow stronger every time they break off and grow back.

Pokémon
BLACK & WHITE
QUIZ
WELCOME TO MY HUMBLE ABODE!
Slam
SLAM
HWOOOSH...
Bye...
HWOOOSH...
LEAVING... ALREADY?
IT'S MUCH WARMER OUTSIDE!
Which of these Dragon-type Pokémon weighs the least?
1
Kyurem
2
Druddigon
3
Hydreigon

Unova Pokédex No.131
BISHARP
Too Bad, 1
Quiz answer for page 55.
Answer 2
Kyurem weighs 716.5 lbs., Hydreigon weighs 325.7 lbs. and Druddigon weighs the least at "only" 306.4 lbs.
I'M BISHARP, THE BADDEST GUY EVER!!
OH, YOU ARE, ARE YOU?!
I HATE TO BRAG, BUT...
...I'M PRETTY BAD TOO!!
I'll let you team up with me—if you're bad enough!

POKÉMON BLACK & WHITE QUIZ
IS THAT SO...?!
HEH HEH HEH... WELL, I LEFT THE DINNER TABLE WITH-OUT ASKING TO BE EXCUSED!
AND I DIDN'T BRUSH MY TEETH BEFORE GOING TO BED!
Heh heh heh...
UM...YEAH... SORRY. DON'T NEED ANY HELP AFTER ALL! NOPE! OKAY THEN... BYE NOW!!
Shoo! Scram!
H-HUH ...?
Which of these moves would be most effective against Bisharp?
1
Poison Jab
2
Psychic
3
Brick Break

HEATMOR

A Burning Secret

Quiz answer for page 57.

Answer 3

Bisharp is a Dark- and Steel-type Pokémon, so Poison- and Psychic-type moves have no effect on it, but a Fighting-type move would be super effective against it.

THAT'S BETTER. ♡
Sh loop
Tied in a knot
NOW FLAMES CAN'TSPURT OUT OF YOUR MOUTH...
GRMMPHH... HMMPH... (BUT NOW I CAN'T TALK!)
POKéMON BLACK & WHITE QUIZ
Heatmor is Durant's natural enemy. How do Heatmor defeat Durant?
1
They capture the Durant using their sticky tongue.
2
They poke Durant with their sharp claws.
3
They burn through Durant's steel shell with their flame-covered tongue.

Unova Pokédex No.119
CUBCHOO
Cold Comfort
Quiz answer for page 59.
Answer 3
Heatmor sucks in oxygen through the hole in its tail to generate a flame inside its body.
WATCH OUT, OSHA-WOTT! YOU'RE STANDING ON THIN ICE!
YOU COULD FALL THROUGH!
COME UP HERE WHERE IT'S SAFE.
OKAY, BUT...
HOW DO I GET UP THERE ...?!

BLOOP
CLIMB UP MY SNOT!!
BLOOOOOOOOOP
Uh... I'm good... Thanks...
POKÉMON BLACK & WHITE QUIZ
Cubchoo's Ability is Snow Cloak. What does it do?
1
Turns the weather into a hailstorm during battle.
2
Raises Cubchoo's evasion in the Hail weather condition.
3
Prevents Cubchoo from getting burned.

DRUDDIGON

Losing Face

Quiz answer for page 61.

Answer 2

When in the Hail weather condition, the hail will not damage a Pokémon with the Snow Cloak Ability. The effect of ① is Snow Warning and ② is Water Veil.

POKéMON BLACK & WHITE QUIZ

Druddigon cannot move when it is cold. How does Druddigon warm up?

1. By bathing in lava at a volcano.
2. By hanging out with a group of Pansear.
3. By absorbing sunlight with its wings.

SWADLOON

A Real Windfall

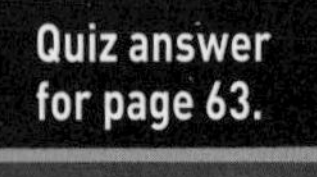

Quiz answer for page 63.

Answer 3

YOU KNOW WHAT, OSHA-WOTT...?
I SWEAR, I'M TOTALLY GOING TO... NNGH!
WHEN THAT LAST LEAF FALLS...
Y-YOU LOOK SO SERIOUS ALL OF A SUDDEN!

Druddigon warms up by absorbing sunlight with its wings.

Pokémon
BLACK & WHITE
QUIZ
Poink
...I'M TOTALLY GOING TO PIG OUT ON THIS PILE OF LEAVES!
SWADLOON REALLY LOVES AUTUMN.
munch munch munch
Whumpf
Swadloon is a dual-type Pokémon. Which of these is also a dual-type Pokémon?
1
Accelgor
2
Escavalier
3
Maractus

Unova Pokédex **No.046**

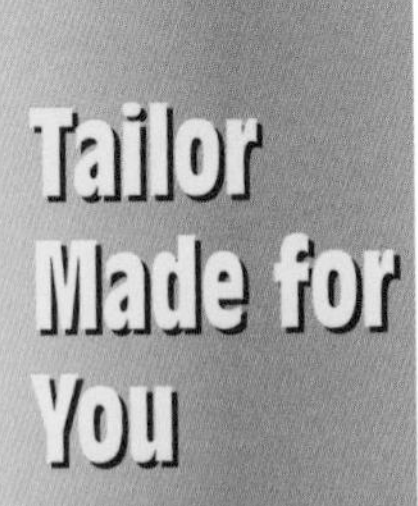

SEWADDLE

Tailor Made for You

Quiz answer for page 65.

Answer **2**

Escavalier is a dual-type Pokémon that is both a Bug type and Steel type.

Pokémon
BLACK & WHITE
QUIZ
PRETTY PLEASE ?!
OKAY ...
A FEW DAYS LATER...
THIS ISN'T QUITE WHAT I HAD IN MIND...
I THINK IT SUITS YOU.
Which Pokémon is lighter than Sewaddle?
1
Pidove
2
Tympole
3
Litwick

UNFEZANT

A Ticklish Situation

Quiz answer for page 67.

Answer 1

Sewaddle is 5.5 lbs. Pidove is the lightest at 4.6 lbs., Tympole is 9.9 lbs. and Litwick is 6.8 lbs.

A MALE UNFEZANT SHAKES ITS FEATHERS TO FRIGHTEN ITS OPPONENT.
shake
Hiss
SSS

POKéMON
BLACK & WHITE
QUIZ
shake shake
shake shake shake
HUH? I DON'T GET IT...
WHY ARE YOU LAUGHING? I'M SUPER SCARY!
tickle tickle
tickle tickle
WOW
Huh?
Because it tickles! Teeheehee!
YOUR TERRIFY-ING DISPLAY IS JUST TICKLING WOOBAT... SIGH.
Which of the following is true about Unfezant?
1
They are very popular since they are friendly to everybody.
2
The female is taller than the male.
3
The females are better at flying than the males.

Unova Pokédex No.086

DUCKLETT

A Friend in Need

Quiz answer for page 69.

Answer 3

The flying abilities of female Unfezant surpass those of the males. The males have plumage on their head.

POKÉMON BLACK & WHITE QUIZ
I DROPPED MY FRUIT IN THE POND.
WOULD YOU GET IT FOR ME?!
'Cause I can't swim...
blub blub
EVERYBODY IS ALWAYS ASKING ME FOR HELP BECAUSE I CAN DO BOTH...
SIGH...
HEY!
WHY DON'T YOU TWO...
...WORK IT OUT TOGETHER?!
Can fly.
Can swim.
What?
But it's easier to ask you...
Ducklett's Ability is either Keen Eye or Big Pecks. Which of these Pokémon also has the Keen Eye Ability?
1
Patrat
2
Mandibuzz
3
Sandile

SWOOBAT

Keep Me Hangin' On

Quiz answer for page 71.

Answer 1

I CAN FLY IN A DARK CAVE.

AND I CAN HANG OFF OF ANYTHING WITH MY TAIL.
click click

Patrat's Ability is either Keen Eye or Run Away.

UM... THAT'S MY NOSE.
SWAYSWAY
EEEEK!
PARDON ME...
POKéMON BLACK & WHITE QUIZ
Swoobat attacks with Assurance. Which of these Pokémon would it be super effective against?
1
Litwick
2
Sawk
3
Swadloon

MIENFOO

Snappy Moves

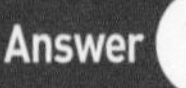

Quiz answer for page 73.

Answer 1

Assurance is a Dark-type move, so it would be super effective against Litwick, a Ghost-type Pokémon.

EMOLGA, OUR STRING SNAPPED...
NOW WE CAN'T PLAY WITH OUR TIN-CAN TELEPHONE ANYMORE!
GO AWAY BEFORE I SNAP AT YOU!
POKÉMON BLACK & WHITE QUIZ
Mienfoo's Ability is Regenerator. What does it enable Mienfoo to do?
1
It automatically heals Mienfoo of status conditions after withdrawing from battle.
2
It restores a little HP after withdrawing from battle.
3
It transforms into a different shape when it gets into trouble.

MIENSHAO

What a Drip

Quiz answer for page 75.

Answer 2

① is the effect for Natural Cure. ③ is the effect for Zen Mode.

Pokémon
BLACK & WHITE
QUIZ
Oh!
My hands are all dirty!
HEY! CUT THAT OUT! I'M NOT A TOWEL!!
BUT I HAVE TO WIPE THEM OFF...
fwf fwf
Mienshao's Jump Kick would be super effective against which of these Pokémon?
1
Golett
2
Sigilyph
3
Roggenrola

GOTHORITA

I'm Your Puppet

Quiz answer for page 77.

Answer 3

Jump Kick is a Fighting-type move. It is super effective against Roggenrola, a Rock-type Pokémon.

BE CAREFUL!! GOTHORITA'S HYPNOSIS IS VERY POWERFUL!!
OF COURSE... THAT'S RIGHT... I DID... ♡
Heh Heh... ♡
AND NEXT... YOU WILL CLEAR THE TABLE FOR ME...
ZZZZ...
jog jog jog
IF THIS KEEPS UP, YOU'LL BE WASHING THE DISHES TOO—AND THANKING GOTHORITA FOR DOING THEM!
Pokémon BLACK & WHITE QUIZ
Gothorita controls people and Pokémon with hypnosis. What category of Pokémon is it?
1
Devious Pokémon
2
Manipulate Pokémon
3
Drowsing Pokémon

GOTHITA

A Matter of Perspective

Quiz answer for page 79.

Answer ②

Gothorita is the Manipulate Pokémon. ① is Purrloin and ③ is Musharna.

GOTHITA CAN SEE INTO THE FUTURE...
COULD IT BE...? DID I JUST SEE... THE END OF THE WORLD?!
The end of the world? That's scary!
THERE IT IS AGAIN !!
THE DARK-NESS!
OH...
blink
WHA-?! GOTHITA IS JUST BLINK-ING!!
POKéMON BLACK & WHITE QUIZ
These Pokémon are the same height as Gothita. Which one weighs the least?
1
Gothita
2
Shelmet
3
Venipede

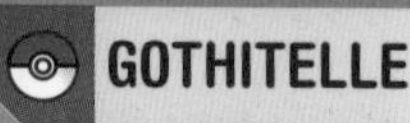

GOTHITELLE

Maid for Service

Quiz answer for page 81.

Answer 3

Gothita is 12.8 lbs., Shelmet is 17.0 lbs., and Venipede is 11.7 lbs., making it the lightest of the three.

I MADE UP YOUR BED FOR YOU ALREADY.
YOU'RE HUNGRY, AREN'T YOU?
YOU MUST BE SLEEPY, RIGHT?
YOU HAVE A BATTLE TOMORROW, DON'T YOU?
So thoughtful...
HERE'S A HANDKERCHIEF.
YOU CAN USE IT AFTERWARDS TO WIPE AWAY YOUR TEARS.
I STARCHED AND IRONED IT FOR YOU.
WHAT?!
YOU MEAN... I'M GOING TO *LOSE*?!
Handkerchief
POKéMON BLACK & WHITE QUIZ
Gothitelle's Ability is Frisk. What does it enable you to do?
1
Find out what held item your opponent has during battle.
2
Find out what dangerous moves your opponent has.
3
Raises the accuracy of your moves, as well as those of the other Pokémon in your group.

COBALION

A Question of the Heart

Quiz answer for page 83.

Answer 1

Frisk tells you what item your opponent has. Anticipation allows you to do ② and Victory Star enables you to do ③.

POKéMON BLACK & WHITE QUIZ
IT MEANS YOUR HEART IS SLICK AND RAZOR SHARP... LIKE A SWORD!
NO!
Oh?
No, no... It means your heart is shiny like... the underside of a leaf!
flip
You're all...so... wrong...
LIKE A SHINY LEAF? YES, THAT MUST BE IT!!
Cobalion has a body and heart of steel. What category of Pokémon is it?
1
Iron Will Pokémon
2
Justice Pokémon
3
Tenacity Pokémon

GOLETT
It All Adds Up, 1
Quiz answer for page 85.
Answer 1
I HATE TO BRAG, BUT... I'M REALLY GOOD AT MATH!!
YOU ARE, GOLETT?
SO IF YOU HAVE TWO OCCA BERRIES AND ONE PAYAPA BERRY...
...HOW MANY BERRIES DO YOU HAVE ALL TOGETHER?
Cobalion is the Iron Will Pokémon.

POKÉMON BLACK & WHITE QUIZ

These Pokémon are all the same height as Golett. Which one is the heaviest?

1 Golett

2

Fraxure

3

Ferrothorn

PAWNIARD

A Leg Up

Quiz answer for page 87.

Answer 3

Golett is 202.8 lbs. and Fraxure is 79.4 lbs. Ferrothorn weighs 242.5 lbs., making it the heaviest.

BEFORE A BATTLE, PAWNIARD SHARPEN THEIR BLADES ON ROCKS BY THE RIVER.
schnick
schnick
splash
splash
WHOA! I SLIPPED!
OH NO!!
PAWNI-ARD FELL INTO THE RIVER!!

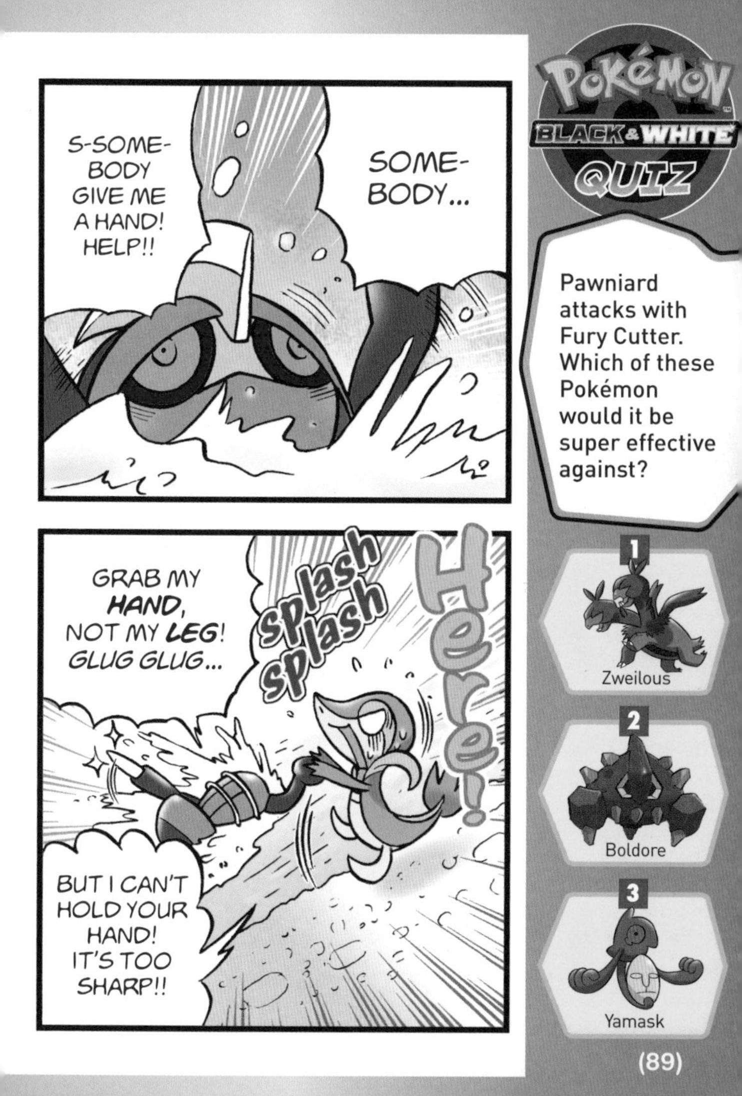
S-SOMEBODY GIVE ME A HAND! HELP!!
SOMEBODY...
GRAB MY HAND, NOT MY LEG! GLUG GLUG...
splash splash
Here!
BUT I CAN'T HOLD YOUR HAND! IT'S TOO SHARP!!
POKÉMON BLACK & WHITE QUIZ
Pawniard attacks with Fury Cutter. Which of these Pokémon would it be super effective against?
1
Zweilous
2
Boldore
3
Yamask

Unova Pokédex No.129
GOLURK
It All Adds Up, 2
Quiz answer for page 89.
Answer 1
Fury Cutter is a Bug-type move. It would be super effective against Zweilous, a Dark-type Pokémon.
Hahaha...
I HATE TO BRAG, BUT I'M MUCH BETTER AT MATH THAN GOLETT. YES-SIREE...
REALLY, GOLURK ...?!
OKAY, SO IF I HAVE ONE PAYAPA BERRY AND TWO OCCA BERRIES...
...AND I SUBTRACT ONE... HOW MANY ARE LEFT?

Pokémon
BLACK & WHITE
QUIZ
YOU KNOW HOW TO SUB-TRACT, RIGHT?
S-SUB-TRACT...?
YOU MEAN LIKE... CUT OUT? LIKE WITH A SAW?
Okay, here goes!
UMM... NOT EXACTLY!
MY BERRIES!
Golurk's move Shadow Punch has no effect on which of these Pokémon?
1
Woobat
2
Rufflet
3
Vullaby

Unova Pokédex **No.033**

WOOBAT

Heartfelt

WOOBAT'S NOSE IS VERY USEFUL!
WOOBAT CAN FLY SWIFTLY EVEN IN THE DARK BY USING ITS ULTRASONIC WAVES.

Quiz answer for page 91.

Answer 2

Shadow Punch is a Ghost-type move. It will not affect Rufflet, a Normal-type Pokémon.

schtuck

WOOBAT USES ITS NOSE TO STICK ITSELF TO A PLACE TO SLEEP.

ZZZ...

WHEN MORNING COMES...
AHH... I FEEL SO RESTED AND RE-FRESHED!
shuffle shuffle
BEWARE, LEST YOU BECOME THE NEXT VICTIM OF WOOBAT'S SUCTION-CUP NOSE!
Ahh...!
WHAT A BEAUTIFUL MORNING!
WOOBAT LEAVES A HEART SHAPE WHEREVER IT ATTACHED ITS NOSE FOR THE NIGHT!
POKÉMON BLACK & WHITE QUIZ
Woobat and Pidove are the same weight. Which one of them is taller?
1
Woobat
2
Pidove
3
They're the same height.

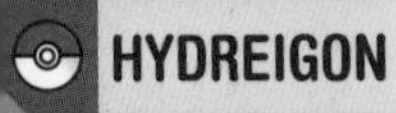

HYDREIGON

Harm in Arm

Quiz answer for page 93.

Answer 1

Woobat is 1'04" and Pidove is 1'00". So Woobat is taller.

WERE YOU WAITING LONG?
Sorry...
THAT'S ALL RIGHT.

I'VE ALWAYS DREAM-ED OF...
... WALKING ARM IN ARM WITH MY DATE.

POKéMON
BLACK & WHITE
QUIZ
...ARM
IN
ARM...
Which of these
Pokémon has
Hydreigon's
Ability
Levitate?
1
Yamask
2
Klink
3
Cryogonal
AN ARM...
WITH A
MOUTH?!
IT WASN'T
QUITE
THE WAY
GOTHITELLE
HAD
PICTURED
IT...

Unova Pokédex No.091
DEERLING
The Four-Season Diet
Quiz answer for page 95.
Answer 3
Cryogonal is the one with the Ability Levitate.
SPRING, THE SEASON OF ROMANCE...
HOW CUTE!
AND SUMMER, THE SEASON TO BE LAZY...
DO YOU LIKE MY NEW COLOR?
I THOUGHT YOU LOOKED DIFFERENT SOME-HOW...

AUTUMN, THE SEASON OF THE HARVEST...
NOTICE ANY-THING NEW?
YOU'VE CHANG-ED COLOR AGAIN!
AND WINTER...
...'cause of all the yummy food I ate all autumn!
I gained a few pounds...
NOW *THAT'S* A *CHANGE*!!
POKéMON BLACK & WHITE QUIZ
When hit by a Grass-type move, what does Deerling's Sap Sipper Ability do?
1
Enables it to regain HP.
2
Boosts its attack.
3
Boosts its defense.

TYNAMO

Two, Four, Six, Eight... Who Do We Interrogate?

Quiz answer for page 97.

Answer 2

Deerling's attack gets a boost when it is hit by a Grass-type move without receiving any damage.

yak yak yak yak
HEY, IS IT TRUE YOU'VE GOT A CRUSH ON ALOMO-MOLA?!
HAVE YOU TOLD ALO-MOMOLA HOW YOU FEEL?!
HOW ARE YOU AND ALOMO-MOLA GET-TING ALONG ?!
H-HOW DO YOU KNOW ABOUT THAT?!
Aiiieeee!
wait! we still have ques-tions!
THEY BOMBARDED CARRACOSTA WITH QUESTIONS!
POKéMON BLACK & WHITE QUIZ
Compared to the other Pokémon in the Unova Pokédex, Tynamo is which of the following...?
1
The smallest
2
The lightest
3
The smallest and the lightest

Unova Pokédex No.109
EELEKTRIK
Double Take
Quiz answer for page 99.
Answer 2
Tynamo is the lightest Pokémon in the Unova Pokédex.
EELEKTRIK IS VERY AGILE NOW THAT IT HAS EVOLVED.
WHOOSH
HEY, WHAT'S THAT?!
POINK
WHOOSH
NO, OVER THERE!
HA HA HA!
THERE'S NOTHING THERE! YOU'RE JUST TESTING MY AGILITY!

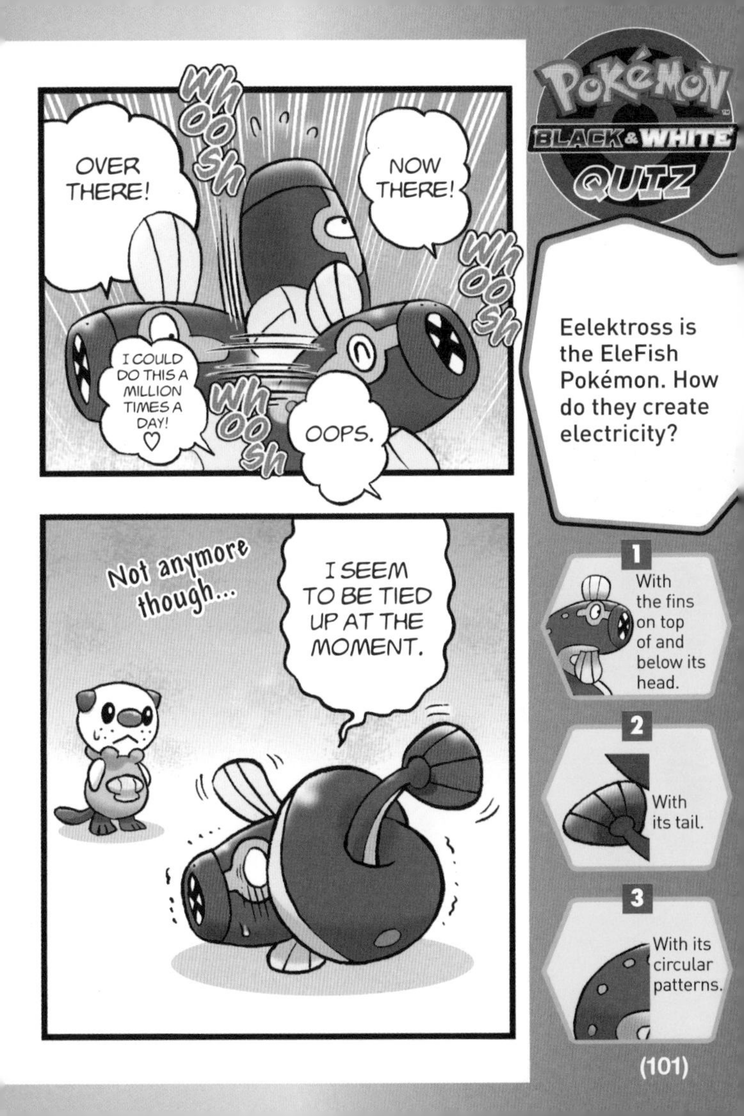
POKÉMON BLACK & WHITE QUIZ
WHOOSH
OVER THERE!
NOW THERE!
WHOOSH
I COULD DO THIS A MILLION TIMES A DAY! ♡
WHOOSH
OOPS.
WHOOSH
Not anymore though...
I SEEM TO BE TIED UP AT THE MOMENT.
Eelektross is the EleFish Pokémon. How do they create electricity?
1
With the fins on top of and below its head.
2
With its tail.
3
With its circular patterns.

EELEKTROSS

Humor ...Fail!

Quiz answer for page 101.

Answer 3

The circular patterns are Eelektross' electricity-generating organs. They press the pattern onto their opponents to electrify them.

Rrr...
...iiiiiippp
So much fun! ♥
See? ♥
YEAH... NOW YOU CAN TEAR UP THE JOKES YOU WROTE THAT AREN'T FUNNY...
POKéMON BLACK & WHITE QUIZ
Eelektross' Ability is Levitate. What does it provide full immunity to?
1
Electric-type moves
2
Ground-type moves
3
Flying-type moves

ZWEILOUS

A Turning Point

Quiz answer for page 103.

Answer 2

Levitate is an Ability that provides full immunity to Ground-type moves.

POKÉMON BLACK & WHITE QUIZ

The following Pokémon are the same height as Zweilous. Which one is the heaviest?

1

Zweilous

2

Sawk

3

Mienshao

BLITZLE

Haiku Decision

Quiz answer for page 105.

Answer 2

Zweilous is 110.2 lbs., Sawk is 112.4 lbs. and Mienshao is 78.3 lbs., so Sawk is the heaviest.

Pokémon
Black & White
Quiz
Phew
Aaa-hhh...
glug glug glug
Lemon-ade
THAT WAS A NO-BRAINER!
GASP GASP... GOOD IDEA...
(HAIKU)
THE WHITE AND THE BLACK...
NOT CHOOSING BETWEEN THE TWO...
IT IS ALWAYS RIGHT.
Which of these statements about Blitzle is true?
1
They generate electricity with their front legs when they run.
2
They catch lightning with their mane and store the electricity.
3
When they emit electricity, the stripes on their body glow.

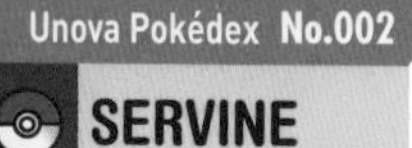

A Room with a Smell

I CAN'T SEE ANYTHING THROUGH ALL THIS GRASS...

SLASH SLASH SLASH

AIR CUTTER !!

SLASH

Quiz answer for page 107.

Answer 2

When the sky is covered with thunderclouds, Blitzle appear to catch the lightning with their manes.

POKéMON BLACK & WHITE QUIZ
THE GRASS WAS SHIELDING GARBODOR'S NEST...
HOW DARE YOU!
BLECH...
Yuk
THIS IS AN INVASION OF PRIVACY!
This is what Servine's tail looks like. Whose tails are these?
1
2
3
SERVINE CUT THE GRASS.
GARBODOR CUT THE CHEESE.
THIS IS AN INVASION OF MY NOSE!
Stinky...
BLECH

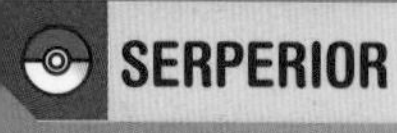

SERPERIOR

Equal Time

Quiz answer for page 109.

Answer

① is Pansear, ② is Pansage, and ③ is Archeops. Could you tell?

BUT I'M BATTLING YOU NOW...
...SO THAT MEANS I'M WORTHY, RIGHT?
JUST KID-DING...
SMACK
FLOOSH
This is so beneath me...
SERPERIOR GAVE THAT ATTACK ITS ALL.
POKÉMON
BLACK & WHITE
QUIZ
Serperior is a dignified Pokémon who only gives its all when facing a worthy opponent. What category of Pokémon is it?
1
Proud Pokémon
2
Formidable Pokémon
3
Regal Pokémon

CHANDELURE

It Followed Me Home...

Quiz answer for page 111.

Answer 3

Serperior is a Regal Pokémon. ① is Unfezant and ② is Samurott.

Creeeekk
I BETTER GET INTO MY HOUSE, QUICK!!
dash
Eeeeeeeek.
Aaaccckkk!
CHANDELURE WAS DEFEATED BY A DOOR. KNOCK ON WOOD!
POKÉMON BLACK & WHITE QUIZ
What does Chandelure burn to create its flames?
1
Spirits
2
Fear
3
Jealousy

ESCAVALIER

Chivalry Is Not Dead

Quiz answer for page 113.

Answer 1

Chandelure absorbs spirits and then burns them to create its flames.

POKÉMON BLACK & WHITE QUIZ

Which of the following is true about Escavalier?

1. They wear the same shell Shelmet wore.
2. They hop around their opponent and attack with their lances.
3. When confronted with a powerful opponent, they run away.

SIGILYPH

Drawing the Line

Quiz answer for page 115.

Answer 1

Escavalier evolves from Karrablast when traded for Shelmet, and keeps Shelmet's shell.

POKÉMON
BLACK & WHITE
QUIZ
WHAT ?!
THIS CIRCLE IS YOUR TERRITORY...?
IT'S TINY!!
YES... EVERYTHING OUTSIDE OF THAT CIRCLE IS MY TERRITORY!!
WAIT... YOU DON'T MEAN...?!
Huh?!
It is said that Sigilyph used to guard something. What was it?
1
An ancient temple
2
The graves of an ancient people
3
An ancient city

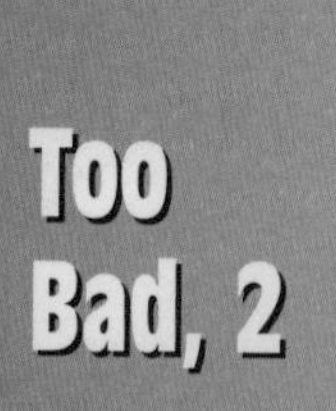

Too Bad, 2

Quiz answer for page 117.

Sigilyph still remember when they guarded an ancient city. They fly along the same route.

EMOLGA AND OSHAWOTT WERE PLAYING WITH A TIN-CAN TELEPHONE...
...AND I STEPPED ON THE STRING!
Huh? I can't hear you.
Hello...?
Hello ...
SIGH... BUT THAT'S NOT THE KIND OF THING YOU MEANT, IS IT...?
Whoa...
THAT'S PRETTY DARN EVIL!!
EVEN I CAN'T DREAM UP MEAN THINGS TO DO LIKE THAT!
POKéMON BLACK & WHITE QUIZ
What qualities do Scrafty look for when choosing the leader of their group?
1
A strong kick
2
A loud voice
3
The largest crest

SCRAGGY

Keeping up Appearances

Quiz answer for page 119.

Answer 3

Scrafty choose their leader based on the size of their crest.

HEY!!
WHO WANTS A BERRY?!
Me, me, me!
ME, ME, ME!
shloompf
Looks like food is everything to you!
POKÉMON BLACK & WHITE QUIZ
Which of the following is true about Scraggy?
1
It pulls up its baggy skin to stay warm.
2
It is good at kick attacks.
3
It has a very thick skull.

SWANNA

Dance Like No One Is Watching

Quiz answer for page 121.

Answer 3

Scraggy has an incredibly thick skull.

?!
glow glow
Heh heh...
snicker snicker
AAAAARGH!
YOU TRICK-ED ME !!
Dawn comes several times a day when I'm around!
Ha Ha Ha Ha Ha
Wahhhh!
POKÉMON BLACK & WHITE QUIZ
What distinguishes the leader of a flock of Swanna from the others?
1
It has the longest neck.
2
It dances in the center.
3
It has the loudest cry.

ZEKROM

Get a Real Charge Out of It, 1

Quiz answer for page 123.

Answer 2

Swanna begin dancing at dawn. The one in the middle is the flock's leader.

Pokémon
BLACK & WHITE
QUIZ
zzzt
zzzt
zzzt
zzzrrrrt
zzzort
W-WHY ...?!
I SAID CHEER UP!
NOT CHARGE UP!
OOPS... SORRY...
cough cough
Zekrom's Ability is Teravolt. What does it enable Zekrom to do?
1
To use its moves regardless of its opponent's Ability.
2
To use its opponent's moves.
3
To boost its Special Attack when struck by an Electric-type move.

ZEBSTRIKA

Get a Real Charge Out of It, 2

I GOT ELECTRIFIED!
sigh...
NOW I'M THE ONE WHO NEEDS CHEERING UP!!

Quiz answer for page 125.

Answer 1

I WONDER WHAT'S WRONG WITH SCRAGGY ...?
HE DOES LOOK A LITTLE RUN DOWN...
I CAN RE-CHARGE HIS BATTERIES!

Zekrom's Teravolt enables it to use its moves regardless of its opponent's Ability.

POKéMON
BLACK & WHITE
QUIZ
Zebstrika attacks with Discharge! Which of these Pokémon does it have no effect upon?
1
Emolga
2
Rufflet
3
Landorus
ZZZt
ZZZt
ZZZt
ZZZt
YOW!
E-Electricity again...
JUST LEAVE ME ALONE! PLEASE!
zzt zzt
HUH? DIDN'T HE WANT TO GET CHARGED UP?
Uh... Probably not.

Now You See It...

Quiz answer for page 127.

Answer 3

Discharge is an Electric-type move. It has no effect against Landorus, a Ground-type Pokémon.

POKÉMON BLACK & WHITE QUIZ
WELL? WHAT DO YOU THINK?
OF WHAT? WHEN ARE YOU GOING TO SHOW ME YOUR TRICK?
I ALREADY AM! THIS TRICK IS CALLED "STAY!" OH... I SEE YOU KNOW "ROLL OVER"...
Zorua's Ability is Illusion. What does it do?
1
Lowers the opponent's accuracy.
2
Enables Zorua to disguise itself as the last Pokémon in the party.
3
Prevents an opponent from inflicting a critical hit.

ZOROARK

Putting the Pow in Powerful

Quiz answer for page 129.

Answer 2

When it joins a battle it comes out disguised as the last Pokémon in the party.

POKÉMON BLACK & WHITE QUIZ
MAKE AN IMAGE OF ME!
OOH OOH!
Woot woot woot
I CAN'T DO THAT!!
Huh?
I CAN ONLY CREATE ILLUSIONS OF POWERFUL POKÉMON.
Hey!
What are you implying?!
Zorua is a Tricky Fox Pokémon. What category of Pokémon is Zoroark?
1
Wily Fox Pokémon
2
Evil Fox Pokémon
3
Illusion Fox Pokémon

SAMUROTT
Overdoes It
Quiz answer for page 131.
Answer 3
Zoroark is the Illusion Fox Pokémon.

HEY, SAMUROTT!
WHICH WAY DID OSHAWOTT GO...?

shhhnk

THAT WAY... I THINK...
WHOA! YOU DON'T HAVE TO DRAW YOUR SWORD!
Sure it's cool, but... You could just point!

50 PERCENT SURE...
WAIT... YOU'RE NOT EVEN *SURE*?!

POKéMON
BLACK & WHITE
QUIZ
These Pokémon are the same height as Samurott. Which one is the heaviest?
1
Samurott
2
Seismitoad
3
Krookodile

SAWK

Pleased as Punch

YIPPEE! YAY!
I'M SO MOVED, SO TOUCHED ...

Quiz answer for page 133.

Answer 3

I JUST CAN'T HELP PUNCHING THINGS WHEN I'M HAPPY!
IS THAT SO, SAWK...?

Samurott is 208.6 lbs. and Seismitoad is 136.7 lbs. At 212.3 lbs., Krookodile is the heaviest.

Ta-dah!
LOOK AT THIS! I'M SO HAPPY BECAUSE GOTHORITA GAVE ME A PRESENT!
kathunk
crrunch
WAHHHH ?!
POKÉMON BLACK & WHITE QUIZ
When do Sawk get angry?
1
When they lose their belt.
2
When they lose a battle.
3
When somebody disturbs their training.

GARBODOR

In the Eye of the Beholder

Quiz answer for page 135.

Answer 3

Sawk get angry when you disturb them during training.

Pokémon Black & White Quiz

Garbodor attacks with Gunk Shot! Which of these Pokémon does this move have no effect upon?

1. Venipede
2. Larvesta
3. Durant

DUOSION

Noodling Around, 1

Quiz answer for page 137.

Answer 3

Gunk Shot is a Poison-type move that has no effect upon Durant, a Steel-type Pokémon.

POKéMON BLACK & WHITE QUIZ
Whizz
AAAAA-AAAH!!
SUDDENLY, THE OTHER BRAIN DECIDES TO DO SOMETHING DIFFERENT!
bang
Duosion have two brains. What category of Pokémon are they?
1
Mitosis Pokémon
Come and watch me dance!
LET'S DANCE!
2
Double Pokémon
BUT... I'M HUN-GRY...
clap clap clap clap clap clap clap clap
3
Brain Pokémon

AUDINO

What Makes You Tick

Quiz answer for page 139.

Answer 1

As the Mitosis Pokémon, when Duosion's two brains are thinking the same thing, they can unleash their maximum power.

I'M AUDINO.
IF I STRETCH OUT THE FEELERS ON MY EARS, I CAN HEAR REALLY WELL!

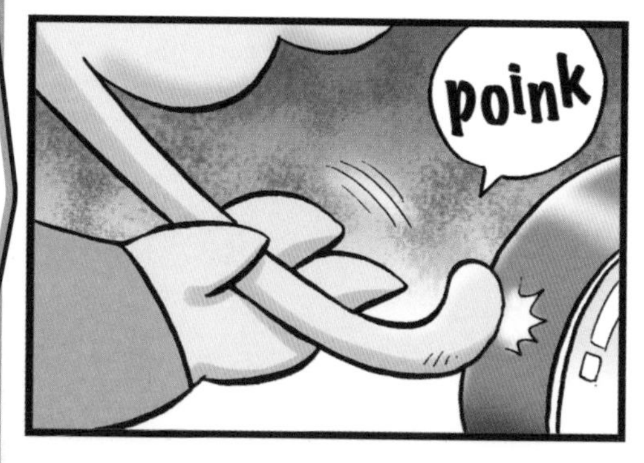

poink

POKéMON
BLACK & WHITE
QUIZ
OH NO... I DON'T HEAR A THING!!
THE CLOCK ISN'T TICKING!
WAHHH!
I'VE LOST MY HEARING!
OR THE CLOCK IS JUST OUT OF BAT- TERIES...
Audino has the Healer Ability. What does it do?
1
It restores a little HP when it is withdrawn from battle.
2
It heals its own status condition when it is withdrawn from battle.
3
It can heal an ally's status condition.

FOONGUS

Noodling Around, 2

HEY! I LOOK LIKE...
...YOU-KNOW-WHAT, DON'T I?

Quiz answer for page 141.

Answer 3

OH! A POKÉ BALL...
RIGHT?
NOPE! I LOOK LIKE...

The Healer Ability can sometimes heal an ally Pokémon's status condition.

POKéMON BLACK & WHITE QUIZ

Foongus' Ability is Effect Spore. What does it do?

1

Lowers the accuracy of Poison- and Grass-type moves.

2

Poisons, paralyzes, or puts the opponent to sleep.

3

Heals Foongus' HP when they are poisoned.

DARUMAKA

Put on the Brakes

Quiz answer for page 143.

Answer 

When Foongus receive a direct attack, their opponent may receive a Poison, Paralysis or Sleep status condition.

GREEN LIGHT...
push push push push
RED LI...
URGH ...
RED LIGHT! RED LIGHT!
YOU NEED TO GO TO TRAFFIC SCHOOL!!
POKéMON BLACK & WHITE QUIZ
Which of the following is not true about Darumaka?
1
A flame burns inside its body.
2
It transforms when weakened in battle.
3
The flame inside it shrinks when it is asleep.

ROGGENROLA

What's in a Name?

Quiz answer for page 145.

Answer 2

Darumaka does not transform in battle. Darmanitan is the Pokémon who transforms when weakened in battle. It hardens into a stone-like form called Zen Mode.

NOW I REMEMBER...!
IT'S... PURSE!
Aaaaargh.
ker-rrack
I'm sorry. So sorry!
THE ANSWER IS... CURSE.
POKÉMON BLACK & WHITE QUIZ
Which of these moves is super effective against Roggenrola?
1
Sand Tomb
2
Rock Tomb
3
Sludge Wave

PIGNITE

Feeding the Flames

Quiz answer for page 147.

Answer 1

Roggenrola is a Rock-type Pokémon, so Sand Tomb, a Ground-type move, is super effective against it.

Ta-dah!
OH, ALL RIGHT! HELP YOURSELF TO THIS YUMMY GARBAGE THEN!
GARBAGE?! YOU'RE OFFERING ME GARBAGE FOR A SNACK?!
ULP! WELL... AT LEAST YOU'VE GOT ENOUGH RAGING ENERGY TO BEAT DRUD-DIGON NOW...
POKÉMON BLACK & WHITE QUIZ
What does Pignite emit when it is in trouble?
1 Fire
2 Smoke
3 Poison gas

Unova Pokédex No.054
PETILIL
Open Sesame
Quiz answer for page 149.
Answer 2
Pignite emits smoke when it is in trouble.
COME ON... YOU LOST THE BATTLE, BUT... YOU DON'T HAVE TO BE ALL DEPRESSED ABOUT IT!
I MEAN, LOOK AT YOU! THE LEAVES ON YOUR HEAD HAVE ALL WITHERED...
Petilil's leaves close up when it is unhappy!!
I KNOW!
I'LL LEND YOU A FUNNY COMIC BOOK TO CHEER YOU UP!
I'LL GO GET IT NOW. HOLD ON A SEC...
IT'LL HAVE TO BE REALLY FUNNY TO GET MY LEAVES TO OPEN UP. SIGH...

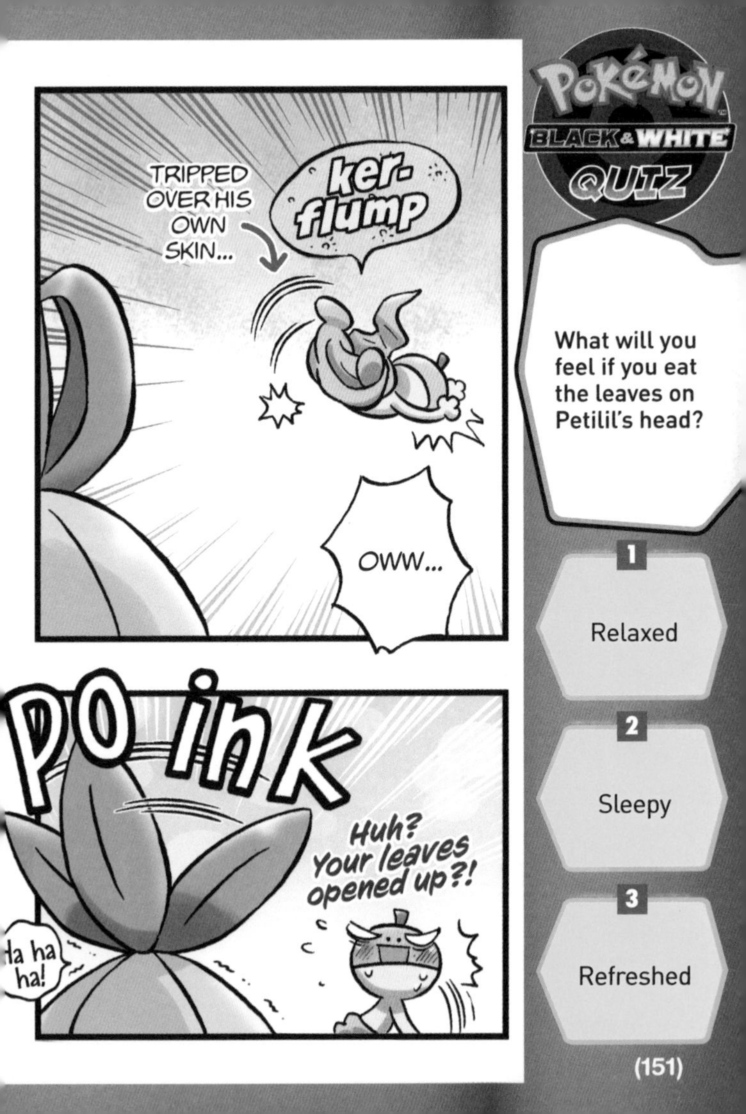
POKÉMON
BLACK & WHITE
QUIZ
TRIPPED OVER HIS OWN SKIN...
ker-flump
OWW...
POINK
Huh? Your leaves opened up?!
Ha ha ha!
What will you feel if you eat the leaves on Petilil's head?
1
Relaxed
2
Sleepy
3
Refreshed

SHELMET

Tongue Twister Trap

Quiz answer for page 151.

Answer 3

Eating the leaves on Petilil's head will refresh you!

...FOUR SHEL...
...merff !!
I BIT MY LIP!!
hop hop hop hop
LOOKS LIKE YOUR TONGUE HAS MET ITS MATCH...
POKéMON BLACK & WHITE QUIZ
What category of Pokémon is Shelmet?
1
Snail Pokémon
2
Shell-On Pokémon
3
Shell Pokémon

PURRLOIN

A Feat of Feet

Quiz answer for page 153.

Answer 1

Shelmet is the Snail Pokémon.

WHOOSH
WHOOSH
WHOOSH
WHOOSH
YOU CAN PLAY WITH A HULA HOOP ON FOUR FEET TOO!!
WHOOSH
WHOOSH
WHOOSH
WHOOSH
HEY, YOU'RE RIGHT!
WHOOSH
WHOOSH
WHOOSH
BUT IT'S HARDER THIS WAY...
TRY YOUR EARS...
POKÉMON BLACK & WHITE QUIZ
Which of these is the same type of Pokémon as Purrloin?
1
Minccino
2
Zorua
3
Stunfisk

MINCCINO

Unmasking the Truth

Quiz answer for page 155.

Answer 2

Purrloin is a Dark-type Pokémon. Zorua is also a Dark-type Pokémon.

*SEE THE WOOBAT COMIC ON PAGE 92.

Which of these is not true about Minccino?

1. They like to keep clean.
2. They use their cute looks to trick people into trusting them and then steal from them.
3. They greet each other by rubbing their tails together.

CINCCINO

Roughing It

Quiz answer for page 157.

Answer 2

Stealing things is a characteristic of Purrloin, not Minccino.

Pokémon
Black & White
Quiz
CINCCINO IS AWOKEN BY...
HEY...
CINCCINO WILL NEVER TAKE THEM CAMPING AGAIN!
nuzzle
nuzzle
ZZZ ZZZZ ...
ZZZ ZZZZ ...
I'M A POKÉMON, NOT A BLANKET!!
Cinccino is what category of Pokémon?
1
Scarf Pokémon
2
Neckpiece Pokémon
3
Chinchilla Pokémon

SNIVY

Don't Be Nosy

Quiz answer for page 159.

Answer 1

The correct answer is Scarf Pokémon. It's Minccino who is the Chinchilla Pokémon.

DID YOU EAT SOMETHING SOUR?
I TOLD YOU, THAT'S MY NOSE!!
That's why your face is all scrunched up, huh?
AND I'M GOING TO MAKE YOU POUT IF YOU DON'T STOP IT...!!
Ha ha ha! Stop, that tickles!
poke
POKÉMON BLACK & WHITE QUIZ
What happens to Snivy when they aren't feeling well?
1
They turn yellow.
2
Their tail droops.
3
They burrow under-ground and fall asleep.

Unova Pokédex No.120
BEARTIC
When Push Comes to Shove
Quiz answer for page 161.
Answer 2
Snivy's tail droops down when it isn't feeling well.
TH-THOSE ARE SOME SHARP-LOOKING CLAWS YOU'VE GOT THERE!
WHAT?! ARE YOU MAKING FUN OF ME?!
ER...
UH...
N-NO! I WOULD NEVER DO THAT!!

Har har
har har
har!
pat
pat
pat
pat...
AWW... DID I SCARE YOU?!
I KNOW. I WAS JUST TEASIN' YA.
SWOOOOSSh
VANILLITE SLID ABOUT 700 FEET...
OOPS ...
smack!
POKÉMON BLACK & WHITE QUIZ
Beartic freezes its breath to make a weapon to fight with. What do they make?
1
Fangs and claws of ice
2
A huge ball of ice
3
A huge icicle

Unova Pokédex No.069

COFAGRIGUS

Well in Hand

GRR...
fwoop
T-TEPIG! LOOK UP!!

Quiz answer for page 163.

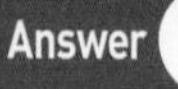
Answer 1

Beartic freezes its breath to create fangs and claws out of ice.

I DON'T KNOW, BUT S-SOME-THING'S CLINGING TO THE CEILING ABOVE US BY ITS LEGS!!
I-IS THAT A GHOST?!

WRONG!!
boing
I'M CLINGING TO THE CEILING...
Yeek!
...WITH MY HANDS!!
Ha!
POKÉMON BLACK & WHITE QUIZ
What is Cofagrigus' body covered with?
1
Oil used in the mummification process
2
Pure gold
3
Desert sand

YAMASK

A Hearty Apology

Quiz answer for page 165.

Answer 2

Cofagrigus love gold nuggets. Their bodies are covered in pure gold.

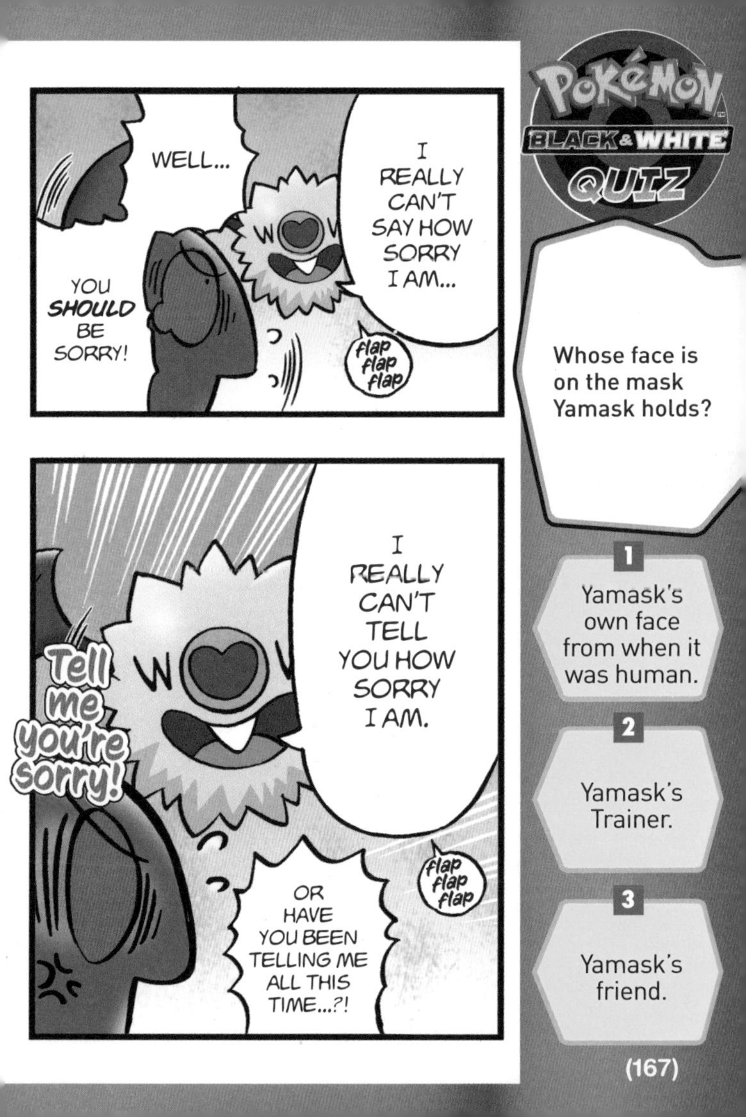
WELL...
I REALLY CAN'T SAY HOW SORRY I AM...
YOU **SHOULD** BE SORRY!
flap flap flap
I REALLY CAN'T TELL YOU HOW SORRY I AM.
Tell me you're sorry!
OR HAVE YOU BEEN TELLING ME ALL THIS TIME...?!
flap flap flap
POKÉMON BLACK & WHITE QUIZ
Whose face is on the mask Yamask holds?
1 Yamask's own face from when it was human.
2 Yamask's Trainer.
3 Yamask's friend.

FERROSEED

A Real Gem

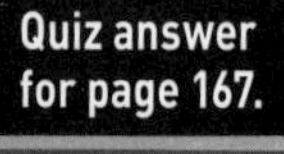

Quiz answer for page 167.

Answer 1

The mask is the face of Yamask from when it was human. Sometimes they look at their mask and cry.

Pokémon Black & White Quiz
GIVE ME ONE TOO!
whoosh whoosh whoosh
Ferroseed is covered with spikes. How do they move around?
1
By rolling.
OH. IT'S JUST A BERRY. TOO BAD.
What do you mean, just a berry?!
2
By shooting out their spikes. This propels them in the opposite direction.
I THOUGHT YOU SAID BERYL...
FERROSEED ABSORBS MINERALS FROM ROCKS.
(BERYL IS A TYPE OF MINERAL.)
Awesome!
3
By floating in the air using Psychokinesis.

TERRAKION
Give It Up
Quiz answer for page 169.
Answer 1
Ferroseed move by rolling around.
Smack
Smack
GRRR... THE SODA WON'T COME OUT... IT'S STUCK!
TERRAKION HAS PHENOMENAL POWER!
MOVE ASIDE!
FEEBLY WHACK-ING THE MACHINE WON'T DO ANY GOOD!

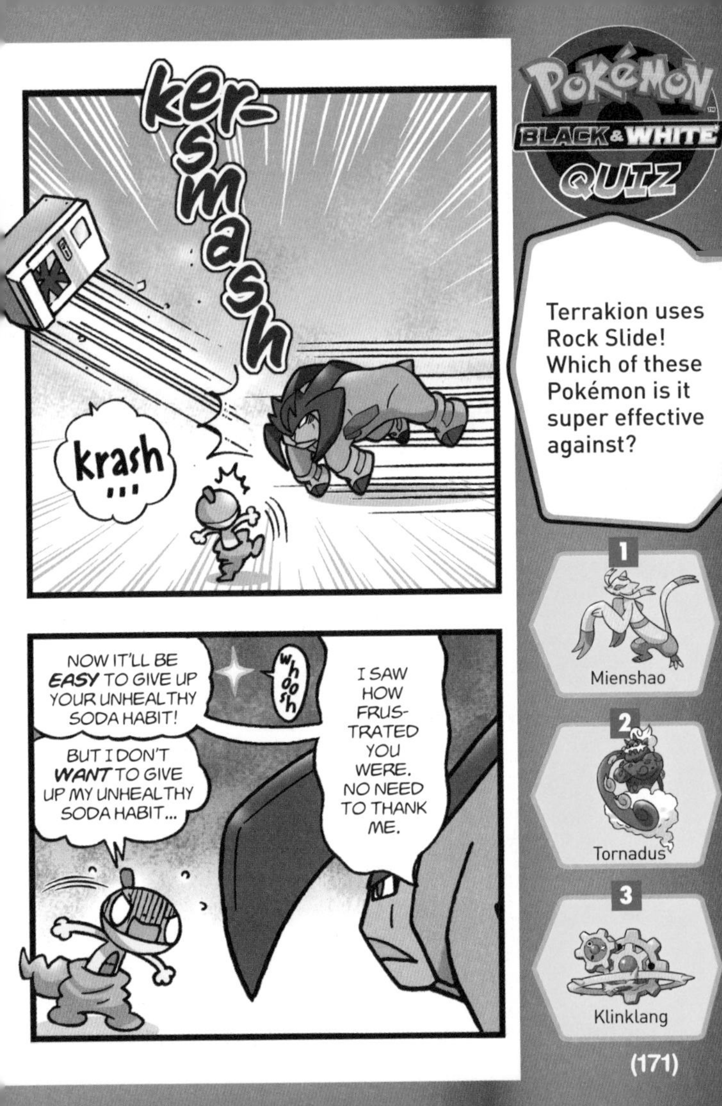
ker-smash
krash
...
POKéMON
BLACK & WHITE
QUIZ
Terrakion uses Rock Slide! Which of these Pokémon is it super effective against?
1
Mienshao
2
Tornadus
3
Klinklang
NOW IT'LL BE EASY TO GIVE UP YOUR UNHEALTHY SODA HABIT!
whoosh
I SAW HOW FRUS-TRATED YOU WERE. NO NEED TO THANK ME.
BUT I DON'T WANT TO GIVE UP MY UNHEALTHY SODA HABIT...

GALVANTULA

The Eyes Have It

Quiz answer for page 171.

Answer 2

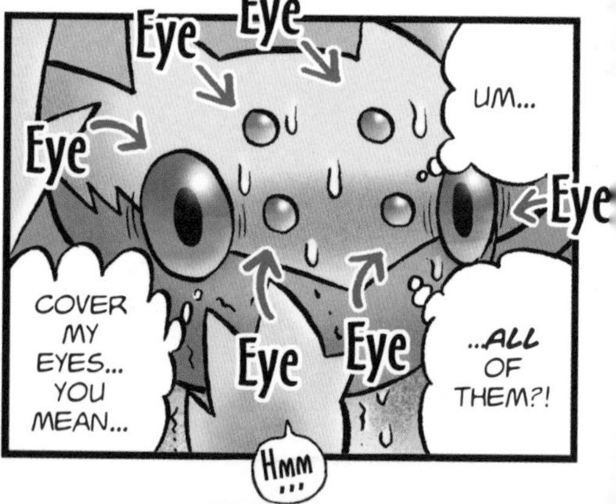

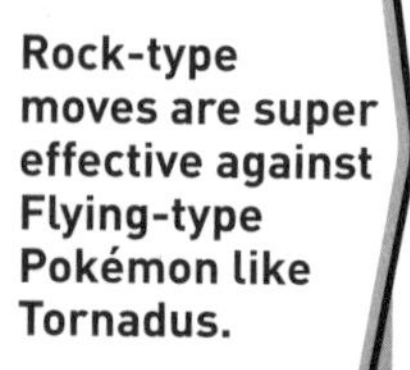

Rock-type moves are super effective against Flying-type Pokémon like Tornadus.

Crackle
crackle
Crackle
krak
krak
krek krek
Owww...
WHAT HAPPENED?!
LEG CRAMPS...
POKéMON BLACK & WHITE QUIZ
What does Galvantula use to capture its prey?
1
An electrically charged web
2
A sticky web
3
A poisonous web

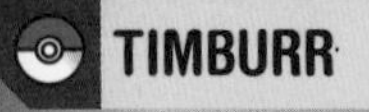

TIMBURR

Knock, Knock on Wood

Quiz answer for page 173.

Answer 1

Galvantula use an electrically charged web to electrify their prey.

WHOK
WHO'S THERE ?!
Oww oww
AND MORE OWW...
I MUST BE HEARING THINGS...
HUH? NO ONE'S HERE.
POKÉMON
BLACK & WHITE
QUIZ
Where do Timburr often appear?
1
Construction sites
2
Martial arts schools
3
Wrestling rings

Unova Pokédex No.039
GURDURR
Emotional Roller-coaster
Quiz answer for page 175.
Answer 1
Timburr appear at construction sites to help out.
STEEL BEAMS...
...ARE REALLY USEFUL FOR MAKING FRIENDS.
YOU CAN USE THEM FOR A SLIDE...
OR A SEESAW...
Whee! Whee!
Ha ha ha ha... Yay!

Why do Gurdurr carry a steel beam everywhere they go?

1

To help construct buildings.

2

To have something to eat when they're hungry.

3

To build their upper-body strength.

EXCADRILL

Can You Dig It?

EXCA-DRILL, YOU LOOK SO STRONG AND COOL...

Quiz answer for page 177.

Answer 3

AND *YOU* LOOK LIKE A TOTAL CRY-BABY...
HEY! THAT WAS MEAN! WHY ARE YOU TAKING A DIG AT ME?

Gurdurr carry steel beams to help them work out and to show off their muscles to their comrades.

DIG? WHY, THAT'S WHAT I DO BEST!
clink clink
WATCH ME!
chunk chunk
cha-ching
BZZZZZZ....
TRANS-FORM!!
YOU CAN'T DIG YOUR WAY OUT OF THIS!
thud thud thud thud thud
POKÉMON BLACK & WHITE QUIZ
Excadrill dig their nests more than 300 feet below the surface. What category of Pokémon are they?
1 Under-ground Pokémon
2 Subterrene Pokémon
3 Mole Pokémon

TORNADUS

Rain, Rain, Go Away...

Quiz answer for page 179.

Answer 2

Excadrill is the Subterrene Pokémon. Drilbur is the Mole Pokémon.

Pokémon Black & White Quiz
karaaaack!
I CAN'T HEAR EXACTLY WHAT THEY'RE SAYING THROUGH ALL THIS WIND, RAIN AND THUNDER...
rummmbbl!
BUT CLEARLY THE POKÉMON BELOW ARE RAISING THEIR VOICES IN PRAISE!
hwooooosssh
SO I'LL MAKE AN EVEN **BIGGER** STORM FOR THEM!
They must be cheering me on!
rumble...
HEY! STOP IT!
GO HOME !!
YOU'RE RUINING OUR LAUNDRY!
Which of the following types of moves has no effect upon Tornadus, a Pokémon who can create huge storms?
1
Ground type
2
Electric type
3
Water type

Unova Pokédex **No.055**

LILLIGANT

Quiz answer for page 181.

Answer 1

Tornadus is a Flying-type Pokémon, so Ground-type moves have no effect upon it.

POKÉMON BLACK & WHITE QUIZ
LILLIGANT...
GUESS WHAT? I HAVE A DATE!
Blue
Red
Green
Yellow
WHAT COLOR TIE SHOULD I WEAR?
A TIE MAKES A GOOD IMPRESSION, DON'T YOU THINK?
Sigh...
The fragrance of the flower on Lilligant's head has a special effect on others. What does it do?
1
Relaxes you.
2
Makes you sleepy.
3
Cheers you up.

THROH • 1
Belt It Out, 1
Quiz answer for page 183.
Answer 1
The fragrance of Lilligant's flower has a relaxing effect.
THROH SEEMS REALLY DE-PRESSED...
THROH HAVE NO ENERGY WITHOUT THEIR BELT.
I HEAR HE LOST HIS BELT.
HIS... BELT?
OBVIOUSLY THROH'S BELT.

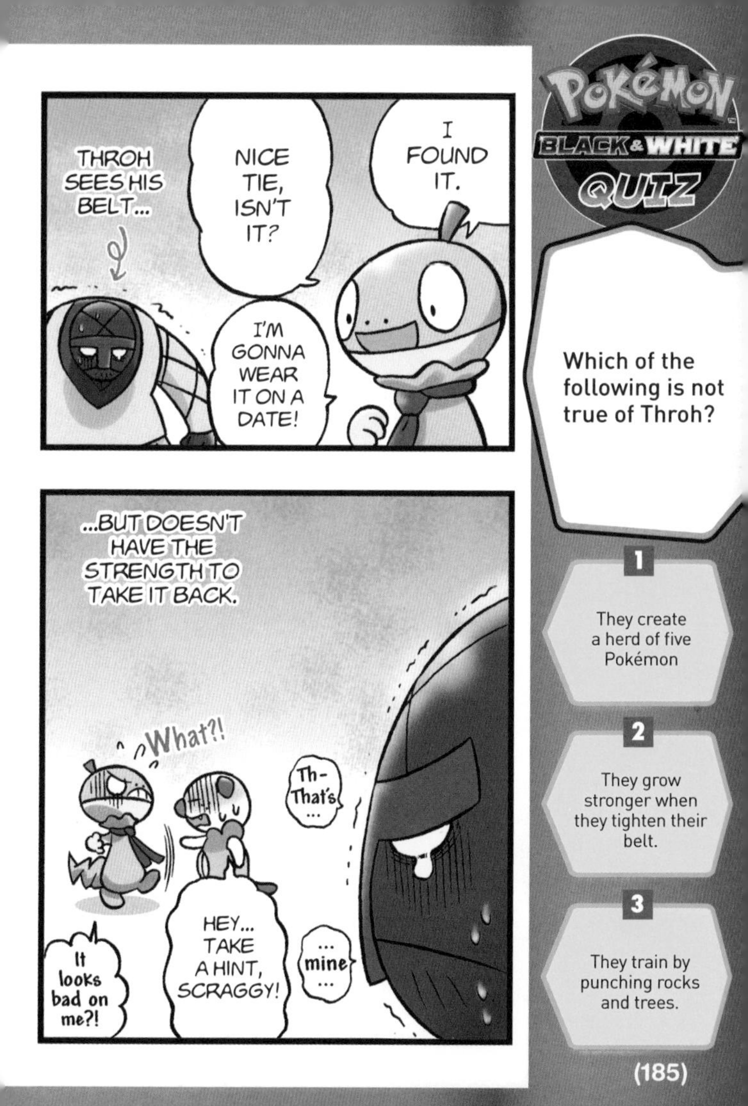
POKÉMON BLACK & WHITE QUIZ
I FOUND IT.
NICE TIE, ISN'T IT?
THROH SEES HIS BELT...
I'M GONNA WEAR IT ON A DATE!
...BUT DOESN'T HAVE THE STRENGTH TO TAKE IT BACK.
What?!
Th-That's...
...mine...
HEY... TAKE A HINT, SCRAGGY!
It looks bad on me?!
Which of the following is not true of Throh?
1
They create a herd of five Pokémon
2
They grow stronger when they tighten their belt.
3
They train by punching rocks and trees.

THROH • 2

Belt It Out, 2

NOW THAT THROH HAS TIED HIS BELT BACK ON...
...HE'S ALL POWERED UP AGAIN!!
skwnnk!

THANKS FOR EXPLAINING THINGS TO SCRAGGY, OSHAWOTT.

SURE. I'M GLAD YOU HAVE YOUR BELT BACK.

I'm grateful.

Quiz answer for page 185.

Answer 3

Throh does not train by punching rocks and trees. The Pokémon that trains that way is Sawk.

WHERE IS SCRAGGY?
HUH? COME TO THINK OF IT...
HELP... ME...
Whoops! I was so eager to put my belt back on, I forgot to take it off Scraggy first!
pant pant
POKÉMON BLACK & WHITE QUIZ
What do wild Throh use to make their belts?
1
Vines
2
Zoroark's shed fur
3
Bouffalant's head hair

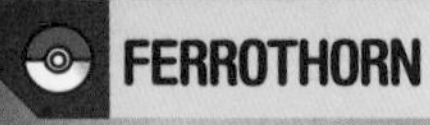

FERROTHORN

Stuck on You

Quiz answer for page 187.

Answer 1

Wild Throh weave vines to create their belt.

EXCUSE ME, FERRO-THORN... WOULD YOU LEND ME A HAND?
HUH...? BUT... I'M STUCK TO THE CEILING...
Really stuck!
I NEED YOU TO HOLD MY FLASHLIGHT FOR A SEC AND SHINE IT DOWN ON MY MAP.
Map
Besides, I don't have a hand... just feelers...
HMPH. SO YOU WON'T HELP ME OUT?
THANKS FOR NOTHING!
POKéMON BLACK & WHITE QUIZ
What category of Pokémon is Ferrothorn?
1
Tri-thorn Pokémon
2
Thorn Pod Pokémon
3
Thorn Seed Pokémon

Unova Pokédex No.013

HERDIER

On the Straight and Narrow

for page 189.

Answer 2

Ferrothorn is the Thorn Pod Pokémon.

Herdier went straight home all right...
IT WAS JUST A FIGURE OF SPEECH!

What special characteristic does Herdier's cape-like fur have?

1

It is very thick and protects them from heat and cold.

2

It is very hard and protects them from attacks.

3

It is very sharp and wounds those who attack it.

VANILLUXE

All for One, and One for All!

HEY, ME...

HEY... I'M GETTING SLEEPY.

I'LL KEEP WATCH SO YOU CAN TAKE A NAP.

ZZZ...

ZZZ...

BUT THEN...IT FALLS ASLEEP.

Quiz answer for page 191.

Answer 2

Herdier's fur is very hard and thus decreases damage it receives.

POKéMON BLACK & WHITE QUIZ
HEY, NOW I'M TIRED! MIND IF I TAKE A QUICK NAP?
NO PROBLEM. I'LL STAND WATCH THIS TIME!
BUT... IT FALLS ASLEEP AGAIN.
ZZZ...
ZZZ...
So they really are one Pokémon after all...
What happens when both of Vanilluxe's heads get angry at the same time?
1
They shoot lumps of ice from both their mouths.
2
They shoot a blizzard from their horn.
3
They create a hailstorm.

SIMISEAR

Too Hot to Handle, 1

Quiz answer for page 193.

Answer 2

They shoot a blizzard from their horn and bury the area in snow.

Mellllt
Free Pops
Intense heat.
It's okay! The stick says I won another one!
It melted ...
YOU CAN'T EAT ICE CREAM EITHER, CAN YOU...?
POKÉMON BLACK & WHITE QUIZ
From what part of its body does Simisear scatter embers during battle?
1
Its head and tail
2
Its mouth
3
Its hands

PANSEAR

Too Hot to Handle, 2

Quiz answer for page 195.

Answer 1

Simisear attacks by scattering embers from its head and tail.

YOU LOOK LIKE YOU'RE DANCING...
A BOMB?!
A BOMB?!
A BOMB?!
Huh?
Heh heh heh
I WAS JUST KIDDING. ♡
FINE.
YOU HAVE THE BERRY. ENJOY!
Hot!
Hot!
Hot!
toss
POKéMON BLACK & WHITE QUIZ
This is what Pansear's tail looks like. Who do the tails below belong to?
1
2
3

It's All in the Eyes, 1

Quiz answer for page 197.

Answer

① is Patrat, ② is Emboar and ③ is Zebstrika.

Pokémon
Black & White
Quiz
YOU'RE ALWAYS BLUE...
AND BY BLUE, I MEAN SAD AND GRUMPY!
What category of Pokémon is Basculin?
I'LL SHOW YOU...
See? I rest my case!
...SAD AND GRUMPY!
splash
splash
splash
AND FOR MY NEXT QUES-TION...
RED- AND BLUE-STRIPED BASCULIN DO NOT GET ALONG.
splash
1
Fighting Pokémon
2
Hostile Pokémon
3
Discord Pokémon

Unova Pokédex No.056

BASCULIN
(RED-STRIPED FORM)

It's All in the Eyes, 2

Quiz answer for page 199.

Answer **2**

Basculin is the Hostile Pokémon.

ARE YOU KIDDING ME?!
YOUR EYES ARE RED FROM **CRYING** BECAUSE YOU'RE ALWAYS LOSING BATTLES!
Har har har har har har
Now you're making me see red!

YES, THE RED- AND BLUE-STRIPED BASCULIN DO NOT GET ALONG AT ALL...

The following Pokémon are the same weight as Basculin. Which one is the tallest?

JOLTIK

Down Under

JOLTIK, YOU'VE GOT FOUR EYES...

Quiz answer for page 202.

Answer 2

Axew is 2'00", Gothorita is 2'04"and Roggenrola is 1' 04". Gothorita is the tallest.

...BUT THERE ARE THINGS EVEN YOU CAN'T SEE, AREN'T THERE?
WHAT ?!

POKéMON BLACK & WHITE QUIZ
I HAVE FOUR EYES, SO MY EYESIGHT IS EXCELLENT!!
HA HA HA! DON'T BE SILLY!
CAN YOU SEE YOUR TUMMY?!
WHOA... YOU'RE RIGHT...
I CAN'T SEE IT...
I'VE NEVER SEEN IT!!
Based on the Unova Pokédex, which of the following is true about Joltik?
1
It is the lightest.
2
It is the smallest.
3
It is the lightest and the smallest.

BOUFFALANT

Hair Today, Gone Tomorrow

HEY, BOUFFA-LANT!!

Quiz answer for page 203.

Answer 2

Joltik's height is 0'04". It is the smallest Pokémon in the Unova Pokédex.

I SAW YOUR BATTLE YESTER-DAY...
THAT WAS A VERY POWER-FUL...
...HEAD-BUTT YOU GAVE OSHA-WOTT!

BY THE WAY... I HAVEN'T SEEN...
...OSHA-WOTT SINCE THEN.
shuffle shuffle
Have you...?
I'M... RIGHT HERE...
Poink
SO ITCHY... I NEED AN OSHA-WOTT COLLAR...
POKéMON BLACK & WHITE QUIZ
The following Pokémon are the same height as Bouffalant. Which one weighs the least?
1
Bouffalant
2
Zoroark
3
Zebstrika

Unova Pokédex No.026

TRANQUILL

Peace Out

HELLO. I'M TRANQUILL. I LOVE PEACE.

I DREAM OF A FUTURE WHERE EVERYONE LIVES IN HARMONY TOGETHER.

WHY ARE YOU PAINTING A CIRCLE ON MY WALL?

H-HEY!!

Quiz answer for page 205.

Answer 3

Bouffalant is 208.6 lbs., Zoroark is 178.8 lbs. and Zebstrika is 175.3 lbs. So Zebstrika is the lightest.

Heh heh

I'M NOT. I'M PAINTING...

...A PEACE SIGN...

...ON YOUR WALL.

I JUST HAVEN'T FINISHED IT YET.

Kidding! It's just a circle!

POKÉMON BLACK & WHITE QUIZ

Which of the following moves has no effect on Tranquill?

1 Shadow Punch

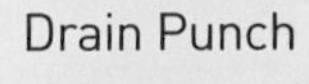

2 Drain Punch

3 Ice Punch

VANILLITE

Chilling with Friends

Quiz answer for page 207.

Answer 1

Tranquill is a Normal- and Flying-type Pokémon, so Shadow Punch, a Ghost-type move, has no effect on it.

It is said that Vanillite were formed from icicles bathed in energy. Where was the energy from?

1 A blizzard's icy wind

2 The morning sun

3 Moonlight

Cracking the Code

Quiz answer for page 209.

Answer 2

Vanillite were formed from icicles bathed in energy from the morning sun.

POKÉMON BLACK & WHITE QUIZ
ting
ting
Quiz Book
Which of the following moves is super effective against Vanillish?
1
Rock Slide
2
Dragon-Breath
3
Avalanche
I CAN'T CRACK THE QUIZZES... UNTIL SOME-BODY CRACKS THE ICE AROUND THEM...
YOU CAN'T MELT MY ICE THAT EASILY!!
It really won't crack...
Now that's Challeng-ing!
Quiz Book
fwoosh

Unova Pokédex No.048
LEAVANNY
And Sew It Goes
Quiz answer for page 211.
Answer 1
Vanillish are Ice-type Pokémon. Rock-type moves, like Rock Slide, are super effective against them.
YAY! THANK YOU FOR MAKING ME A SUIT OF CLOTHES! ♡
OH!
AND THIS IS FOR YOU TOO...
Comic book
IT'S THAT COMIC BOOK I'VE BEEN WANTING TO READ!
Thank you so much!

POKÉMON
BLACK & WHITE
QUIZ
HUH?!
BUT I CAN'T OPEN IT!
What?!
SO YOU WON'T LOSE ANY PAGES.
OH, THAT'S BECAUSE I SEWED IT SHUT.
Sob...
Comic book
These Pokémon are the same height as Leavanny. Which one is the heaviest?
1
Whirlipede
2
Stoutland
3
Gurdurr

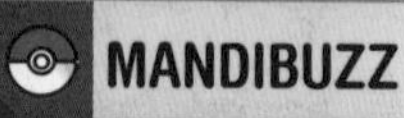

MANDIBUZZ

A Bone to Pick with You

Quiz answer for page 213.

Answer 2

Whirlipede weighs 129.0 lbs., Stoutland weighs 134.5 lbs. and Gurrdurr weighs 88.2 lbs. So Stoutland is the heaviest.

STEEL GIRDERS...
...ARE THE BONES OF A BUILDING, RIGHT?
BUT THEY SURE ARE HARD AND UNCOMFORTABLE TO SLEEP ON!
Cold, too.
POKéMON BLACK & WHITE QUIZ
These Pokémon are the same height as a Mandibuzz. Which one weighs the least?
1
Unfezant
2
Alomomola
3
Mandibuzz

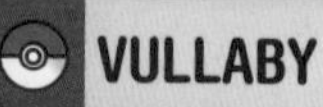

VULLABY

Bowling for Pokémon

Quiz answer for page 215.

Answer 1

Unfezant weighs 63.9 lbs., Alomomola weighs 69.7 lbs. and Mandibuzz weighs 87.1 lbs. So Unfezant is the lightest.

kerrrash!
STRIIIIIKE!
HEY!!
BUT IT'S EASY TO BOWL ON ICE. ♡
Hee hee! ♡
POKÉMON BLACK & WHITE QUIZ
What does Vullaby, the Diapered Pokémon, use to protect its rear end?
1
Bone
2
Egg shell
3
Stone vase

Unova Pokédex No.000

VICTINI

A Born Winner

Quiz answer for page 217.

Answer 1

Vullaby finds a bone, usually a skull, to protect its rear end.

POKéMON
BLACK & WHITE
QUIZ
I THOUGHT WE WERE GOING TO BATTLE!
IF WE PLAY TAG... AND I'M "IT"...
...HOW CAN I...
...HELP YOU BE VICTORIOUS ?!
THERE IS NO "I" IN "TEAM."
Victini is the Victory Pokémon. Which of these characteristics is true of it?
1
Its Ability is Super Luck.
2
It creates an unlimited supply of energy inside its body.
3
It is the Sun Pokémon.

Unova Pokédex No.113

LITWICK

Light at the End of the Tunnel

Quiz answer for page 219.

Answer 2

Victini creates an unlimited supply of energy inside its body.

POKÉMON BLACK & WHITE QUIZ

Litwick attacks with Hex. Which of these Pokémon is it super effective against?

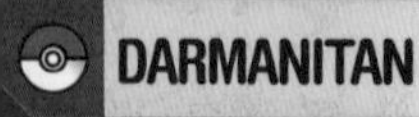

DARMANITAN

Very Punny

Quiz answer for page 221.

Answer 2

Hex is a Ghost-type move, so it is super effective against Yamask, a Ghost-type Pokémon.

POKéMON BLACK & WHITE QUIZ

What does Darmanitan's Zen Mode enable it to do?

1

Become immune to physical attacks.

2

Tackle its opponents with its stone-hard body.

3

Change from Fire type to Fire and Psychic type.

SIMIPOUR

Water Hazard

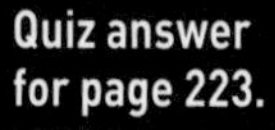

Quiz answer for page 223.

Answer 3

In Zen Mode, Darmanitan's type changes from Fire type to Fire and Psychic type. It becomes a dual-type Pokémon.

Which of these things can Simipour do with its tail?

1

Hang off trees and pick berries.

2

Siphon up and shoot out water.

3

Whip its opponents.

Unova Pokédex No.021

PANPOUR

Do the Recycle

Quiz answer for page 225.

Answer 2

Simipour can siphon up water and shoot it back out with its tail.

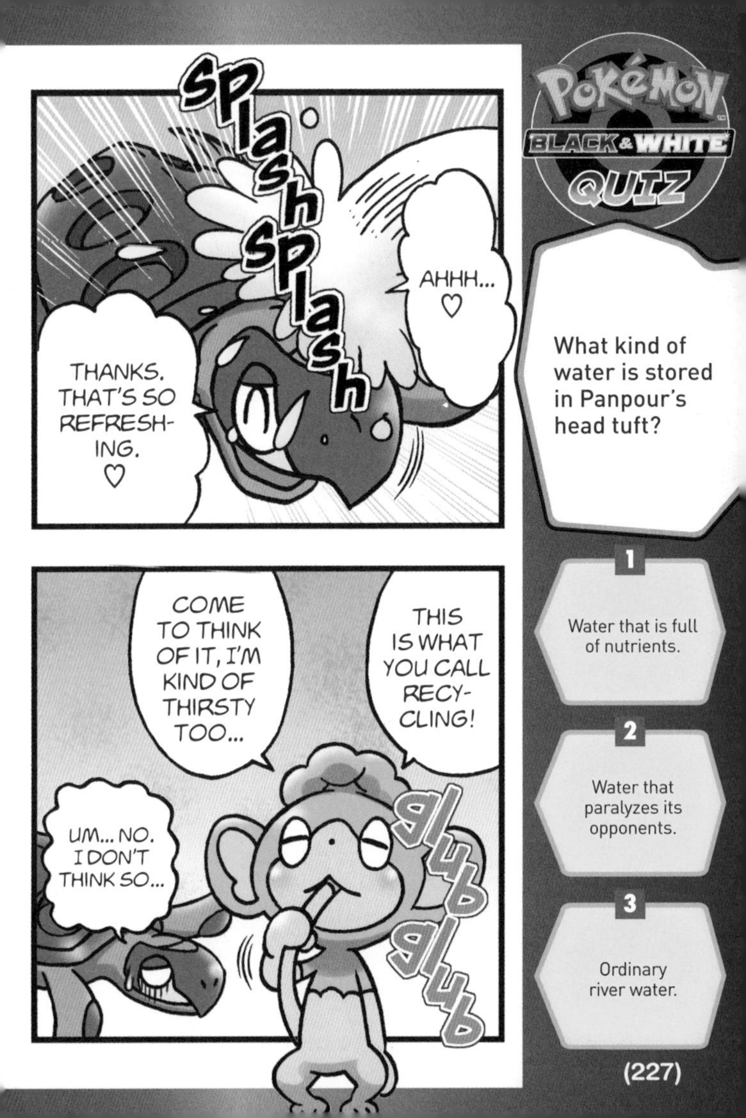
Splash Splash
AHHH... ♡
THANKS. THAT'S SO REFRESH-ING. ♡
THIS IS WHAT YOU CALL RECY-CLING!
COME TO THINK OF IT, I'M KIND OF THIRSTY TOO...
UM... NO. I DON'T THINK SO...
glub glub
POKÉMON BLACK & WHITE QUIZ
What kind of water is stored in Panpour's head tuft?
1
Water that is full of nutrients.
2
Water that paralyzes its opponents.
3
Ordinary river water.

VIRIZION

Help Less

Quiz answer for page 227.

Answer 1

Panpour stores water full of nutrients. Plants watered with this nutrient-rich water grow large.

kerass sh
Aaaaaaaaah...
Oh no...
Wahh...
UM... COULDN'T YOU HAVE HELPED ME IN A LESS DRASTIC WAY?
ummph ummph
Oh dear...
I... can't get up...
CALL FOR HELP!!
POKÉMON
BLACK & WHITE
QUIZ
It is said that Virizion did something significant in the past to protect their friends. What was it?
1
Fought humans.
2
Cut down forests to create fields.
3
Summoned rain to protect them from drought.

VENIPEDE

Falling Flat Footed

Quiz answer for page 229.

Answer 1

Legend has it that Virizion fought against humans to protect its friends.

I FEEL LIKE I'VE FALLEN A HUNDRED FEET!
...
GET IT?! CENTIPEDE POKÉMON?! A HUNDRED? SIGH... I GUESS I PUT MY FEET IN MY MOUTH WITH THAT ONE.
POKÉMON
BLACK & WHITE
QUIZ
These Pokémon are the same height as Venipede. Which one is the heaviest?
1
Venipede
2
Purrloin
3
Shelmet

DEWOTT

Double Trouble

Quiz answer for page 231.

Answer 2

Venipede weighs 11.7 lbs., Purrloin weighs 22.3 lbs. and Shelmet weighs 17.0 lbs. Purrloin is the heaviest.

What does Dewott's Torrent Ability do?

1

Restores HP when it is attacked with a Water-type move.

2

Gradually heals its HP when it is in the Rain weather condition.

3

Powers up Water-type moves in a pinch.

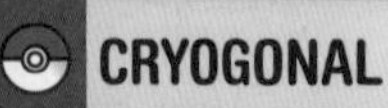

CRYOGONAL

Face Off

Quiz answer for page 233.

Answer 3

When its HP is below one third, Dewott's Torrent Ability makes its Water-type moves stronger.

WHY?!
I ADMITTED DEFEAT, DIDN'T I?!
BUT IT LOOKS LIKE YOU'RE SMIRKING!
HOW CAN YOU TELL I'M SMIRKING WITH THIS FACE?!
POKÉMON
BLACK & WHITE
QUIZ
How do Cryogonal capture their prey?
1
By freezing their prey with their icy breath.
2
By throwing icicles to knock their prey unconscious.
3
By lashing their prey with chains of ice crystals.

FRILLISH

Adrift at Sea

Quiz answer for page 235.

Answer 3

Cryogonal use chains of ice crystals to capture their prey.

ALOMOMOLA ASKED TRANQUILL THE SAME QUESTION.
WHER-EVER THE WIND TAKES ME...
"WHEREVER THE WIND TAKES ME" SOUNDS A LOT MORE ROMANTIC...
TRUTH IS, WE'RE JUST TOO LAZY TO SWIM...
POKéMON BLACK & WHITE QUIZ
Where do Frillish live?
1
Five miles below the surface of the sea
2
Floating on the surface of the sea
3
In a hole on a rocky stretch of beach

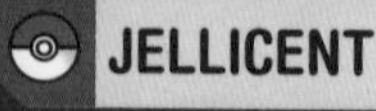

JELLICENT

Don't Talk with Your Mouth Full

Quiz answer for page 237.

Answer 1

Frillish paralyze their prey with poison and drag them five miles below the surface to their lairs.

bloop
bloop
HUH?
I LEFT MY BREAKFAST HERE! AND NOW IT'S GONE!

Pokémon
BLACK & WHITE
QUIZ
DID YOU TWO SEE SOMEONE STEAL MY BREAK-FAST?!
HEY!
bloop
bloop
HEY!
bloop
bloop
THEY CAN'T ANSWER BECAUSE THEIR MOUTHS ARE FULL...
IF ONLY THEY COULD GIVE ME A CLUE...
These Pokémon are similar in weight. Which one is heavier than Jellicent?
1
Druddigon
2
Ferrothorn
3
Garbodor

TIRTOUGA

Punny You Should Ask

Quiz answer for page 239.

Answer 1

Jellicent weighs 297.6 lbs. At 306.4 lbs., Druddigon is heavier than Jellicent. Garbodor weighs 236.6 lbs. and Ferrothorn weighs 242.5 lbs.

POKÉMON BLACK & WHITE QUIZ

Tirtouga was restored from a fossil. About how many years ago did it live?

1 A million

2 Ten million

3 A hundred million

Unova Pokédex No.051

SCOLIPEDE

Fast Talker

Quiz answer for page 241.

Answer 3

Tirtouga swam the ancient seas a 100 million years ago.

ONE WOOBAT SWOONS SOON FOR TWO SWOOBAT.
SEVERAL SNIVY SAT SADLY STARING AT SAWK AND SEWADDLE.
TOLD YOU I WAS FAST!
AT TONGUE TWISTERS! SO WHAT? WHO CARES?!
You try saying them five times fast!
NOTE THAT SCOLIPEDE DOES MOVE FAST TOO...
POKÉMON
BLACK & WHITE
QUIZ
What does Scolipede use to poison its opponents?
1
The horn on its head
2
The claws on its neck
3
The horns on its tail

Unova Pokédex No.050
WHIRLIPEDE
Back Track
Quiz answer for page 243.
Answer 2
It digs its claws into its opponents to poison them.
WHIRLIPEDE DOESN'T MOVE MUCH.
BUT IT CAN BE DANGEROUS IF YOU STARTLE IT!
creep creep
WELL, LOOK WHO'S AT THE CREST OF A HILL...
I THINK I'LL PLAY A LITTLE TRICK ON WHIRLIPEDE!
Guess who?!
whop whop
Huh?!

Aaaaaah!
WOW, YOU SURE SURPRISED ME! HA HA!
Whirr Whirr Whirr Whirr
AND ME... I DIDN'T KNOW YOU COULD ROLL *BACKWARDS*... OUCH.
POKéMON BLACK & WHITE QUIZ
Whirlipede attacks with Poison Tail. Which of the following Pokémon does it have no effect upon?
1 Klink
2 Accelgor
3 Whimsicott

TEPIG

Running Hot and Cold

Quiz answer for page 245.

Answer 1

Poison Tail is a Poison-type move. It has no effect on Klink, a Steel-type Pokémon.

YOU WON'T BE ABLE TO FOCUS WITH A RUNNY NOSE!
I'M FINE!
I DON'T HAVE A RUNNY NOSE... I HAVE A SMOKY SNOUT! ♡
crackle crackle
Pokémon Black & White Quiz
What do Tepig roast with the fire they breathe out of their noses?
1 Leaves
2 Roots
3 Berries

THUNDURUS

A Welcome Surprise, 1

Quiz answer for page 247.

Answer 3

Tepig like to roast berries and eat them.

POKéMON BLACK & WHITE QUIZ
I WENT
ka boom!
RIGHT IN FRONT OF OSHA-WOTT...
...AND STOPPED ITS HICCUPS!
Hmm...
HUH?!
AT LEAST MY HICCUPS STOPPED...
WHAT'S WRONG, OSHA-WOTT? YOU'RE SCORCHED!!
ARE YOU OKAY?
SZZL
SZZL
Where does Thundurus shoot thunderbolts from?
1
The horn on its head
2
The spikes on its tail
3
Inside its cloud

STUNFISK

Going Flat Out

Quiz answer for page 249.

Answer 2

Thundurus can discharge thunderbolts from the spikes on its tail.

POKÉMON
BLACK & WHITE
QUIZ
I'M RIGHT HERE! ♡
POP
WHY ARE YOU INSIDE A DRAWER ANYWAY?
ZWOOP
You're so flat!!
What happens to Stunfisk when it emits electricity?
1
Its skin gets soft.
2
It smiles.
3
It pulls its body up.

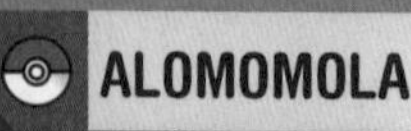

ALOMOMOLA

Play Date, 1

Quiz answer for page 251.

Answer 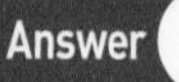 2

Stunfisk smile when they transmit electricity.

SWOOSH
IT'S TIME FOR YOU TO GROW UP!!
HUH? WHERE'D ALOMOMOLA GO...?
WHATEVER. ALOMOMOLA WILL FIND ALOMOMOLA. ♡
HUH?
fwissssh
HELP ME, ALOMO-MOLA!
whoosh
whoosh
whoosh
THERE ARE SOME THINGS EVEN ALOMOMOLA CAN'T DO FOR YOU, YOU NITWIT... LIKE FIND *ITSELF*!!
POKÉMON BLACK & WHITE QUIZ
What effect does the special membrane around Alomomola's body have?
1
It protects it from drying up, even on land.
2
It heals wounds.
3
It prevents its body temperature from falling even in the cold sea.

PIDOVE

Disturbing the Peace

Quiz answer for page 253.

Answer 2

The membrane covering Alomomola's body heals wounds.

Pokémon
BLACK & WHITE
QUIZ
HEY, PIDOVE!
IT'S YOUR TURN TO SWEEP UP TO-DAY.
These Pokémon are the same height as Pidove. Which one weighs the least?
1
Pidove
2
Sewaddle
3
Litwick
HOW CAN THAT BE? I DON'T GET IT...
IT'S SIMPLY BEYOND ME...
Don't you play dumb with me!
Aha ha ha...

MARACTUS
Deserted
Quiz answer for page 255.
Answer 1
Pidove weighs 4.6 lbs., Sewaddle weighs 5.5 lbs. and Litwick weighs 6.8 lbs. So Pidove is the lightest.
THE DESERT IS BURNING HOT...
ARRGH... SO EMPTY...
AND BORING!
Hey!!!
YOU THINK THERE'S NOTHING WORTH SEEING IN THE DESERT?!
HEY! YOU THERE!!

Pokémon Black & White Quiz
cha cha cha
WELL YOU'RE WRONG! YOU CAN SEE... MY DANCE!
WATCH! WATCH! ♡
da da da
THAT'LL COST YOU 100 POKÉMON DOLLARS!
twirl twirl
I DON'T PERFORM FOR FREE, YOU KNOW!
AND NOW MY WALLET'S EMPTY TOO...
Arrrghhh....
Maractus drive away their enemies with their dance and maracas-like sounds. What category of Pokémon is it?
1
Dance Pokémon
2
Maracas Pokémon
3
Cactus Pokémon

OSHAWOTT

Pillow Fight, 1

Quiz answer for page 257.

Answer 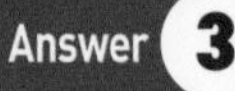

OSHAWOTT NEVER FORGETS TO DO PRACTICE SWINGS THE DAY BEFORE A BATTLE!!
95...
96...

97...
98...
99...
100!
Pant...
Pant...
OKAY. NOW I'M BOUND TO WIN TOMOR-ROW!

Maractus is the Cactus Pokémon. It lives in dry regions.

Pokémon
BLACK & WHITE
QUIZ
THE DAY OF THE BATTLE...
I OVERSLEPT... SORRY!
I worked out too hard yesterday.
...
The scalchop on Oshawott's stomach is made of what substance?
PLUS, I FORGOT MY SCALCHOP...
Ummm...
BUT I BROUGHT MY... ERR... PILLOW?!
How about a pillow fight?!
Let's just cancel...
1
The same material as claws
2
Steel
3
The same material as shells

PATRAT

What Next?, 1

Quiz answer for page 259.

Answer 1

The scalchop on Oshawott's stomach is made from the same material as claws.

WHAT ARE THEY DOING?! ARE THEY PREPARING TO FIGHT ZEKROM OR SOMETHING?
I WANT TO JOIN THEM!!
HALLOOO!
HEY, GUYS! IT'S ME—CUBCHOO!!
WHAT DO YOU THINK?
WHO...?
DOES IT FIT THE CATEGORY?
smack
I think it works.
IS THAT OKAY?
WHAT DO YOU SAY?
I GUESS SO... CUBCHOO ISN'T A POKÉMON TYPE, BUT IT IS A TYPE OF POKÉMON...
HUH...? YOU'RE JUST PLAYING WORD CHAIN?!
POKÉMON BLACK & WHITE QUIZ
Patrat take shifts to maintain a constant watch over their burrows. How do they warn the others of an approaching enemy?
1
With a high-pitched cry.
2
With a signal made with their tails.
3
By rushing back into their burrows.

Unova Pokédex No.011
WATCHOG
What Next?, 2
Quiz answer for page 261.
Answer 2
When Patrat see an enemy, they communicate with one another by using their tails.
I'VE...
...DE-CIDED TO FIGHT ZEKROM!!
WHO ELSE IS IN? WHO'S WILLING TO FOLLOW ME INTO BATTLE?!
clomp clomp
clomp clomp
...ELEC-TRIC...
LET'S TRY AGAIN. ICE...

IT'S NO GOOD.
AH... NUTS.
THERE JUST AREN'T ANY POKÉMON TYPES THAT START WITH A "C."
Ooh!
Let's do what we did last time!
What? Use 'Cubchoo? Again?
Better yet...
How about Crustle?
WILL YOU TWO JUST GO HOME?!
We're not playing Word Chain!
LET'S GO, MINCCINO. I'LL FOLLOW YOU INTO BATTLE TO GET AWAY FROM THESE CLOWNS!!
POKÉMON BLACK & WHITE QUIZ
Watchog threaten their enemies by shining a part of their body. Which part?
1
The pattern on their torso
2
Their eyes
3
The tip of their tails

STOUTLAND

Special Delivery

Quiz answer for page 263.

Answer 1

Watchog threaten their enemies by lighting up the pattern on their body.

POKÉMON BLACK & WHITE QUIZ
LEAVE IT TO ME!
whoooosh
I'll deliver the letter for you.
snag
HUH?!
HEY! DELIVER ME TOO!
Which of these characteristics is not true of Stoutland?
1
They rescue people stranded in snowy mountains.
2
Their long fur protects them from the cold.
3
They like mountains but dislike the sea.

MUSHARNA

Where There's Smoke...

Quiz answer for page 265.

Answer 3

Stoutland likes the mountains and the sea. Stoutland is a wise Pokémon. It rescues people stranded in snowy mountains as well as at sea.

SO THAT'S WHAT THAT "SMOKE" WAS...
IT WAS JUST THE DREAM MIST RISING FROM MUSHARNA.
ZZZ...
NO WONDER I COULDN'T PUT IT OUT!
drip drip

I COULDN'T WAKE UP MUSHARNA EITHER!! HA HA!

Musharna attacks with Psybeam! Which of these Pokémon does it have no effect upon?

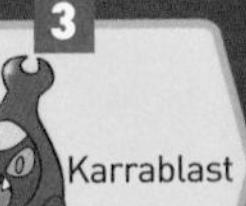

MUNNA

Dreaming of You

Quiz answer for page 267.

Answer 1

Psybeam is a Psychic-type move. It won't have any effect on Liepard, a Dark-type Pokémon.

Munna eats the dreams of both Pokémon and people. What happens when Munna eats a pleasant dream?

1. Munna expels a pink-colored mist.
2. Munna recovers energy.
3. Munna's body shines and it wakes up.

SANDILE

Rotten to the Core

Quiz answer for page 269.

Answer 1

Munna expel pink-colored mist when they eat a pleasant dream.

HEY, YOU!!
NO LITTER-ING!
Don't dirty my dirt!!
DON'T DIRTY MY DIRT! THAT'S A GOOD ONE! ♡
Haha haha ha!
LITTERING IS NO JOKE!
POKÉMON BLACK & WHITE QUIZ
Sandile is a Ground- and Dark-type Pokémon. Which of the following moves has no effect upon it?
1
Force Palm
2
Shadow Ball
3
Thunder-Punch

SAWSBUCK

Fair-Weather Friends

Quiz answer for page 271.

Answer 3

ThunderPunch, an Electric-type move, will have no effect on a Ground- and Dark-type Pokémon like Sandile.

WE DRANK TEA TOGETHER IN THE AUTUMN.
MY FRIENDS ARE SO NICE!
BUT IN THE WINTER... MY FRIENDS DISAPPEARED ...
WE DIDN'T DISAP-PEAR...
WE'RE BURIED UNDER THE SNOW ...
POKéMON BLACK & WHITE QUIZ
What characterizes the leader of a Sawsbuck herd?
1
They are the first to grow plants on their antlers.
2
They can run faster than the others.
3
They have the nicest antlers.

LARVESTA

Tie a Ribbon Round the Pokémon, 1

Quiz answer for page 273.

Answer 3

The Sawsbuck with the most magnificent antlers is the leader of the herd.

ME TOO!! ♡
ME THREE!!!
ME FOUR!!!!
Poink
Poink
SO! HOW MANY RIBBONS DO YOU HAVE TO GO GET NOW?
ACK!
NOT AN ARITHMETIC PROBLEM, ACTUALLY...
I DON'T ***HAVE*** TO GET ***ANY***. GRR...
Ummm...
SORRY. MY **FRIENDS** HAVE NO MANNERS.
POKéMON BLACK & WHITE QUIZ
Which of the following is not true of Larvesta?
1
They live in the desert.
2
When they evolve, their body is engulfed in flames.
3
They shoot fire out of their five horns during battle.

DRILBUR

One for All and All for One

Quiz answer for page 275.

Answer 1

Larvesta do not live in the desert.They live at the base of volcanoes.

Grrrr...
HA! I CAN DO BETTER THAN ONE. I STOLE ALL OF THEM!
My arms are the perfect shape for this, huh?
...THE WHOLE PILE! AND NO FAIR LEAVING BEHIND THE MASTERMIND OF THE PLAN TO FACE THE MUSIC!
I SAID, SNEAK A BERRY, NOT...
whooosh
POKÉMON BLACK & WHITE QUIZ
Cubchoo is the same weight as Drilbur. Which one is taller?
1
Drilbur
2
Cubchoo
3
They are the same height.

DEINO

A Hairy Situation

Quiz answer for page 277.

Answer 2

Drilbur's height is 1'00" and Cubchoo is 1'08". Cubchoo is taller.

POKÉMON BLACK & WHITE QUIZ
HERE.
AND HERE.
YUP. PERFECTLY CLEAR.
Nice emo look too...
Whoa!
Deino's Ability is Hustle. What does it do?
1
Boosts its attack stats but lowers accuracy.
2
Makes it immune to the Sleep condition.
3
Prevents it from flinching.

AMOONGUSS

Show and Tell

Quiz answer for page 279.

Answer 1

Hustle is an Ability that boosts Attack stats but lowers accuracy.

POKéMON
BLACK & WHITE
QUIZ
LOOK!
MANGA!
Super Puns
Puns
LOOK! A TOY!
Amoonguss' Ability is Clear Smog. Which of the following Pokémon is it super effective against?
Look, look!
ARE YOU MIMICKING ME...?!
Lemonade
Lemonade
Puns
Super Puns
1
Snivy
2
Klinklang
3
Purrloin

COTTONEE

Pillow Fight, 2

Quiz answer for page 281.

Answer 1

Clear Smog is a Poison-type move. It is super effective against Snivy, a Grass-type Pokémon.

Pokémon Black & White Quiz

Why do Cottonee shoot out cotton from their bodies when they are attacked?

1. To lighten their body so they can escape faster.
2. Because the cotton is covered with paralyzing spores.
3. As a decoy to distract the enemy.

SIMISAGE

Bully for You

SIMISAGE IS AN ILL-TEMPERED POKÉMON.

HEY YOU! I'M WARNING YOU... GET OFF THAT SWING NOW...

...OR YOU'RE GONNA GET HURT!!!

Quiz answer for page 283.

Answer **3**

HMPH. SIMI-SAGE IS SUCH A BULLY.
CAN'T HE WAIT FOR HIS TURN?!
Get off, I said!!
Come on!

When attacked, Cottonee shoot out cotton to distract their enemy.

How does Simisage battle?

1 With a powerful head-butt attack.

2 By wildly swinging its barbed tail.

3 With rapid-fire punches and kicks.

PANSAGE

The Grass Is Always Greener...

Quiz answer for page 285.

Answer 2

EATING A LEAF FROM PANSAGE'S HEAD RELIEVES WEARINESS.
WHAT'S WRONG...?
YOU LOOK PEAKED.
SO... HUNGRY...
GRRWL
HOLD ON A SEC...
I HEAR THEY'RE SUPER REFRESHING! ♡
Finally, a chance to eat a leaf from Pansage's head! ♡
Heh heh...
SNAP

During battle, Simisage strikes its opponents with its thorn-covered tail.

HERE YOU GO, OSHAWOTT.
ENJOY!
snag
Thanks!
Ugh! It's awfully bitter...
munch munch
GOOD NEWS, OSHAWOTT!
THERE'S LOTS MORE GRASS GROWING OVER HERE.
I'M NOT A BOUFFALANT! I DON'T GRAZE!
Don't you like it, Oshawott?
Bleagh!
snap
POKéMON BLACK & WHITE QUIZ
Pansage's Ability is Gluttony. What does it do?
1
Enables the early use of a held berry.
2
Steals the berry of an opponent.
3
Makes an HP-absorbing move stronger.

TRUBBISH

One Person's Treasure...

Quiz answer for page 287.

Answer 1

Berries are usually used when a Pokémon's HP is greatly reduced, but with the Gluttony Ability Pansage can use them earlier in battle.

WOW! IT'S A JEWEL !!
A VALUABLE TREASURE!
EVERYTHING IS GARBAGE— AND A SNACK— TO TRUBBISH.
SURE IS YUMMY.
Urk
Munch Munch Munch
...
Pokémon Black & White Quiz
Trubbish prefers unsanitary places. What item was this Pokémon created from?
1
Garbage bags
2
Dumpsters
3
Sludge

SOLOSIS

Play Date, 2

PLEASE PLAY WITH ME! ♡

PRETTY PLEASE, WILL YOU PLAY WITH ME?! ♡

Catch!

boink

Ha ha ha ha ha...

Quiz answer for page 289.

Answer 1

Trubbish is a Pokémon created from the chemical reaction between garbage bags and industrial waste.

Pokémon
BLACK & WHITE
QUIZ
rrrrmbl
Ha ha ha!
Which of the following is true of Solosis?
1
They can survive in any environment.
2
They communicate through ultrasonic sound.
3
They fly using their psychic power.
SOLOSIS JUST REALIZED THEY WERE ALREADY PLAYING WITH IT.
OH...!

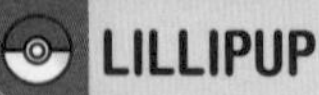

LILLIPUP

Tie a Ribbon Round the Pokémon, 2

Quiz answer for page 291.

Answer 1

Solosis' bodies are encased in a special liquid that enables them to survive in any environment.

POKÉMON BLACK & WHITE QUIZ

Which of the following moves are super effective against Lillipup?

1. Ghost-type moves
2. Normal-type moves
3. Fighting-type moves

REUNICLUS

Shake, Rattle and Roll

WE'LL BATTLE EACH OTHER FAIR AND SQUARE, OKAY? LET'S SHAKE ON IT!

Quiz answer for page 293.

Answer 3

Lillipup is a Normal-type Pokémon, so Fighting-type moves are super effective against it.

HOW ABOUT WE ROLL THAT ROCK AND SEE WHO CAN KNOCK DOWN...
...THE MOST LOGS IN-STEAD?
OKIE-DOKIE!
krumble
Oops! Again...
POKÉMON BLACK & WHITE QUIZ
What happens when two strong Reuniclus shake hands?
1
They arm wrestle.
2
They converse telepathically.
3
They increase each other's psychic power.

LANDORUS

A Welcome Surprise, 2

Quiz answer for page 295.

Answer 3

LANDORUS APPEARS OUT OF THIN AIR!

ARE YOU MAD AT ME?!
YOUR ARMS ARE CROS-SED...
What ...?

When they shake hands, their brains connect, forming a network which increases their psychic power.

POKÉMON BLACK & WHITE QUIZ

When Landorus visits an area, the crops flourish. What is Landorus called?

1 The Guardian of the Fields

2 The Guardian of the Land

3 The Guardian of Crops

LAMPENT

Hanging Around

Quiz answer for page 297.

Answer 1

Landorus is known as the Guardian of the Fields.

I'M LAMPENT.
IT MIGHT NOT SEEM LIKE IT, BUT I'M SCARY.

I'LL SHOW YOU HOW SCARY I AM...
fwap fwap

POKéMON BLACK & WHITE QUIZ
Lampent is an ominous Pokémon. Why does it wander through cities?
1
In search of a long-lost friend.
2
To have fun by scaring people.
3
To find the spirits of the dead.
dash
HUH?
Hey!!!
I'M NOT A CLOTHES HANGER!
Don't mess with me!
Ahahahaha...
Can't take the shirt off by itself.
LAMPENT TAKES ITSELF WAY TOO SERIOUSLY.

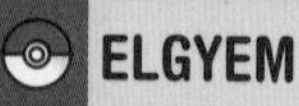

ELGYEM

A Real Pain

Quiz answer for page 299.

Answer 3

Lampent wanders adrift through cities in search of the spirits of the dead.

Pokémon
BLACK & WHITE
QUIZ
MY BACK HURTS...
throb
HUH?!
YOUR BACK? ISN'T THAT YOUR HEAD?
THAT'S FOR ME TO DECIDE!
Where did Elgyem suddenly appear 50 years ago?
1
Deep space
2
Deep below the sea
3
The far reaches of the desert

RESHIRAM

Hung Out to Dry

Quiz answer for page 301.

Answer 3

Elgyem suddenly emerged from the desert half a century ago.

RESHIRAM GETS READY FOR BATTLE...
PREPARE YOURSELF! I SHALL SCORCH YOU WITH MY FLAME!

EXCUSE ME...

LEGEND HAS IT THAT WHEN YOUR TAIL FLARES...
...THE WEATHER CHANGES.
MY LAUNDRY IS HANGING OUTSIDE MY HOUSE...
...SO PLEASE DON'T MAKE IT RAIN, OKAY?
FINE... I'LL WAIT TILL YOU TAKE IT DOWN AND FOLD IT.
POKÉMON BLACK & WHITE QUIZ
These are the three heaviest Pokémon in the Unova Pokédex. Which one is the tallest?
1
Golurk
2
Reshiram
3
Zekrom

Flattery Will Get You Nowhere

Quiz answer for page 303.

Answer 2

Golurk is 9'02", Reshiram is 10'06" and Zekrom is 9'06". The tallest is Reshiram.

LIEPARD... WHAT A UNIQUE BEAUTY YOU ARE!

YOU'RE THE MOST BEAUTIFUL POKÉMON OF THEM ALL!
Ooh...
YOUR RICH FUR... THOSE BEAUTIFUL EYES.
P-PLEASE... PLEASE GO ON A DATE WITH ME!!

SORRY.
I'M ALREADY DATING SOMEONE.
What! You are ?!
THEN...
CAN WE AT LEAST BE FRIENDS ?
DO YOU HAVE A TWIN?
WATCHOG CAN ONLY DREAM...
POKÉMON BLACK & WHITE QUIZ
Liepard attacks with Night Slash. Which of the following Pokémon is it super effective against?

1
Stoutland
2
Sawk
3
Reuniclus

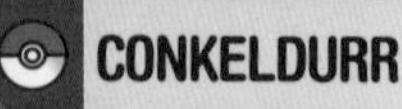

CONKELDURR

A Concrete Plan

Quiz answer for page 305.

Answer 3

Night Slash is a Dark-type move. It is super effective against Reuniclus, a Psychic-type Pokémon.

LOOK! IT'S CONKEL-DURR...
CONK-ELDURR IS USING CONCRETE PILLARS AS WALKING CANES.

AND THAT'S NOT ALL...
poink

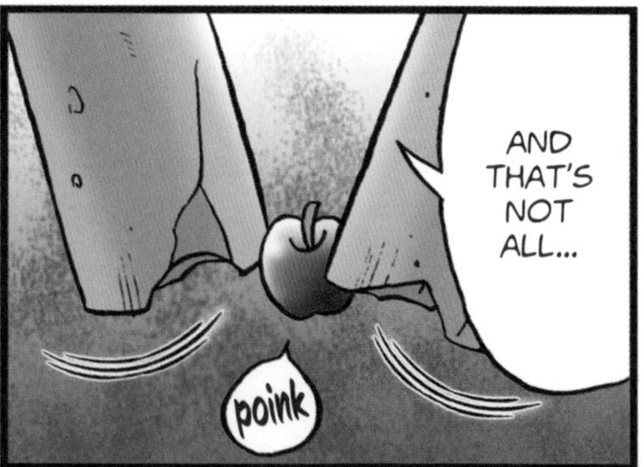